About the Author

LinYi Feng was born in Shanghai, China, during the single child policy period. Growing up in a communist society, he was a national first-class athlete. Next to writing books he is a practising lawyer.

Dog Eat Carrot is his debut book in the English language. *The Brother*, the author's first book, is published in Chinese.

Dog Eat Carrot

LinYi Feng

Dog Eat Carrot

Olympia Publishers
London

www.olympiapublishers.com
OLYMPIA PAPERBACK EDITION

A CIP catalogue record for this title is
available from the British Library.

ISBN: 978-1-80074-319-9

First Published in 2022

Olympia Publishers
Tallis House
2 Tallis Street
London
EC4Y 0AB

Printed in Great Britain

Dedication

To my father

CHAPTER I

I still vividly remember the day I got my bachelor's degree in law; it was the anniversary of the founding of the Communist Party of China. My happiness felt like a cherry blossom in its full and fleeting bloom. After a while it just withered away and died. I hadn't been able to find a job of any kind; my graduation had just led straight into unemployment. My hair grew longer and unkempt, covering my face like a mop. Around that time, I heard some news that made my cherry blossoms come back to life.

One day in August 2004, at the World Athletics Championship, which was dominated by black and white faces, Curly, who had been my friend since our days wearing open-crotch pants, swept in like a whirlwind and became the first Chinese man, the first Asian man and the first Yellow man in history to compete in the one hundred metres final.

Curly looked tanned compared to the white people around him and pale compared to his black competitors. He was six foot three and had long legs and a rather handsome face. His hair was curly and tangled, like instant noodles before adding hot water. His parents were typical Chinese devoid of character and lacking any basis of athleticism that even table tennis could not be played.

When Curly was born, his skin was as dark as a lump of coal. His father found it hard to believe this black baby was supposed to be his and subsequently threatened his wife with divorce. In Chinese tradition, having a son is considered far better than having a daughter. Having a daughter was merely considered better than having a stranger's child, and in the 1980s, family planning was one of the fundamental policies in our country. Only one successful birth was allowed per family, which meant Curly's father wouldn't be able to have another child with his wife even though he loved her deeply.

Curly's mother cried of heartbreak. She asked a doctor if there could have been a mix-up. The doctor said it was impossible and suggested a paternity test to prove it.

Thank God the results confirmed that Curly was not an illegitimate child. His father calmed down and told anybody wondering about his son's dark skin that Curly's mother had had too much soy sauce during her pregnancy, adding it to every single dish whether it was chicken or pigs' feet or anything else. But his wife was not willing to go along with the soy sauce story. She came up with an explanation of her own: A genetic mutation had made Curly's skin dark.

Curly stood on the track of the one hundred metres final. There were eight athletes competing for victory. They came from the USA, Cuba, Jamaica, Lithuania, Canada, Brazil and France.

Before the competition, Curly agreed to give interviews. Reaching the finals however, his expression grew grave. Perhaps he was feeling nervous, because his face looked like he hadn't taken a shit in a whole year.

"My goal for this competition was to reach the finals. Now that I've achieved that goal, I don't feel any pressure any more. I've already written history. I will do my best to perform well, and I hope everyone can lend me their luck and strength," Curly told the television cameras.

At that moment, I was sitting in front of my TV, drinking beer. I couldn't help but sneer. I just thought Curly had watched too much Dragonball Z.

"The stars are bright this evening," the host's voice affectionately issued from the TV. "And Chinese all over the world will be sending their strength and luck to this sincere young man."

The stadium was ablaze with lights, shining and glittering like a big bowl of diamonds in the darkness of the evening. Those in the audience were each a fleck of light inside that bowl, and the whole world — viewers from every nation — watched the live broadcast with expectation. The athletes for the one hundred metres final entered in a line and started their final warm-up.

Thunderous applause rang from every level of the stadium, providing a rhythmic beat for the long jumper who was about to compete. The beat was slow at first, remaining neat and orderly. Then it became faster and faster. Intensity was high. The jumper ended up disappointing the spectators, committing a foul which sent a ripple of groans through the crowd.

Curly wore a Chinese red sports vest and shorts, standing behind the starting block. From the way he was breathing, he looked like a volcano on the brink of eruption. Words that only he could hear teeter-tottered on his lips. He stuck out his arms, pointing out ahead, walked slowly to the block, and crouched down, settling into launch position.

"On your mark..." The referee slowly raised the starting pistol. The whole stadium hushed into such silence that a sneeze could distinctly be heard from one corner.

"Get set..." Eight plump buttocks lifted slowly.

"Bang!" Seven athletes shot forward like arrows, flying towards the finish line. Curly didn't look like an arrow; he looked like a rocket.

"Holy moly!" I yelled about a hundred times, stuttering like

I had a speech impediment. I jumped up from the sofa and almost cut my head on the ceiling fan. I waved my fist in the air until I started breathing like a coffee machine.

Before Curly went to the competition, state-run China Central Television wanted to interview him, and I accepted to join the interview as a guest. I was invited because I was Curly's "best bro" and the eloquent member of our group of athletes. I was needed to help Curly sound corny, and I did say a lot, expressing my opinions in front of the camera. I said this would be the very first time for Curly to participate on the international stage, so we shouldn't put him under too much pressure. This would be an opportunity for him to train and prepare for the next World Athletics Championship, which would be held in Beijing, China. At the right place, with one billion four hundred million people supporting him, Curly would be capable of creating a miracle.

I honestly didn't think that Curly's big moment would come so soon that Autumn. Otherwise, I would have borrowed money from a loan shark to place a bet on him.

After winning the championship, all the headlines were about Curly. He was on TV twenty-four hours a day, and the news about him spread on the internet like a tsunami. People started to gossip about whether he had a girlfriend or not. His parents appeared on TV swearing their son was still single and a virgin.

The total number of women obsessed with Curly seemed to exceed the population of Germany and Belgium combined. In those women's minds, Curly was a real prince.

Journalists all reported the same news without gossip — that Curly was basically an abstinent monk. However, journalists are the most capable hounds in the world and they soon found me. They treated me as though I were the emperor's relative. Nobody had ever treated me like that before. I felt so good that I decided to return the favour by showing them the message that Curly had sent me. I treated them like illiterate children by holding the message up close to their faces and reading it out loud.

Journalists can't stand being treated in such an insulting manner, and in order to prove their literacy, they insisted on reading it themselves: "I'm very good. Girls who do rhythmic gymnastics show their love to me..."

I didn't let them read the whole message. The journalists' faces grew even more desperate. Their eyes were full of greed. I used sincere words in order to say, "Guys, don't get carried away. You have seen the text for yourselves. Seeing is believing."

The very next day, I received the first call from Curly after he won the championship.

"Moshi-moshi?" I said, trying to make my voice like a Japanese geisha.

"Moshi your head," Curly replied, pretending to be angry.

I said, "If you want to moshi my head, it's impossible not to let you moshi my head. But if you don't want to moshi my head, it's impossible to force you to moshi my head. If you—"

"Shut up!" Curly said. "When you were talking to the reporter, what the hell did you say about me?"

"I said you are the most handsome man in the whole universe."

"Listen to me. Keep your mouth shut. Don't say such nonsense to reporters."

"What nonsense did I say?" I asked. "Don't treat a good person badly!"

"If you are a good person, there is no bad person in the world," Curly said. "Stop denying it. I was told what you said and it's been published in the newspaper."

“Which newspaper? And what did it publish?”

“Stop! I have no time to argue with you. Remember, don’t talk to reporters too much. Just wait till I get back to kick your ass.” Curly hung up the phone.

I felt a chill although the temperature was thirty-eight degrees. I ran to the nearest newsstand. From now on, no matter what — even things like sesame mung beans — as long as they were somehow related to Curly, they would make the headlines. The news about him was everywhere. I didn’t need to start going through the newspaper. A black bold headline jumped out at me: “Curly’s best friend spills the beans.” After I read the full story, my face started cramping. I immediately sent a message to Curly.

“Such injustice! That asshole of a reporter distorted the facts. I didn’t say you are dating that girl from the synchronized swimming team. I am going to sue those motherfuckers.”

“Reporters have the brains of thieves. You are no match for them. Control your mouth,” Curly replied.

I learned of Curly’s arrival date from the news. I planned to surprise him by picking him up from the airport. I also invited a beautiful girl named “Kitty” to come along. “Kitty” was just her nickname though she didn’t really look like a kitten. She was just a well-behaved girl, which was rare among athletes. Kitty and I were to meet at the metro station.

“Good morning, Egg Head,” Kitty said to me.

I thought, “What a pretentious child, calling me by my nickname to greet me in the morning.” I started laughing like a dirty pervert and said, “Good morning, Tits.”

Kitty raised her eyebrow and used her fingers to pinch my arm. She pretended to be enraged over my remark and kept pinching. As I saw her twist my flesh clockwise, I squealed like a pig. Kitty was satisfied. She put her nose in the air.

I got a chance to get close to her. I don't know why my eyes automatically glanced at her cleavage. Like a wolf seeing a sheep. Kitty wasn't provocative, but she was always aware of how bouncy her breasts were. As she'd run, her arms would cling to her breasts tightly, and her whole upper body would sway from side to side with her breasts. The coach wanted to correct her movements but failed to do so. By moving that way, she wasn't able to run fast. Our coach felt very sorry for her for having such long legs. It was a waste to let her train for long distance running. Anyway, long distance running doesn't require much speed. She actually could run fast. I saw Kitty run a one hundred metre race once. She ran very fast and her boobs were flying in all directions like a runaway machine gun knocking all her competitors down.

I knew Curly had fancied Kitty before he went to join the national team. That's why I invited her to tag along. I always try to think of others.

On our way to the airport, I told Kitty I had always enjoyed folding paper airplanes and playing with model airplanes. I told her about sitting on some abandoned planes at the amusement park, and about watching all sorts of planes in movies — seeing them take off, land, or even explode — without ever actually taking a flight myself.

"Shame on you," Kitty said.

I shrugged my shoulders and stuck out my lower lip.

When we arrived at the airport, the plane flew over my head. I looked up and my mouth opened by itself. I couldn't help staring. My body was turning in accordance with the planes.

"Oh my God, the plane is goddamn huge!" I cried. "Kitty, could you imagine the feeling of flying in the sky?"

"Don't swear, please!" Kitty said.

"You ought to become a stewardess," I said.

"Where is Curly? Is your information accurate?" Kitty looked around and noticed, "There aren't any reporters or fans here."

To be honest, I wasn't really sure about my information, but I pretended I did.

"Relax, flight delays are very common," I said in a casual tone.

"You're lying through your teeth," Kitty said. "You don't have the experience of flying."

Sometimes Kitty could be serious like a stone.

"You seem to have some complaints," I said. "I may not have much experience flying," my voice grew passionate, "but just like I have never eaten shit before, I still know that shit is stinky!"

Sometimes, I can't endure my own logic. It's especially tough when it's forced.

My stubbornness lost its power as the sun was going down.

CHAPTER II

Curly came to earth a year later than me, his birth completing the Family Planning task of his parents and fulfilling their duty of providing an heir. His father's parents wanted their grandson to be happy and healthy. They hoped that when Curly grew up, he could find a wife who was as kind as his mother and who would also give birth to a son. His father's elder sister swore Curly would have what her son had. Her son and nephew would be the same. Curly's uncle, his father's younger brother, agreed with the notion. He swore what his daughter ate, Curly would also eat. His daughter and nephew would be the same. His parents' expressions didn't seem to agree with him very much. He knew why. He himself has a preference for a son but he lost his chance to have a son, his mood began to wane. His sister found it embarrassing. She spoke for him, "The boy was the palm of a hand, and the girl was back of the hand. They were both flesh."

The whole family's ultimate endeavour was to plant the one root of the generation of Family Planning. As the only son of the male line, they put Curly in their hands for fear of catching cold, put him in their mouths for fear of melting.

Before China transformed from a centrally planned economy into a socialist led market economy, most people were very happy as though it were Utopia. My mother was especially happy. She joined a pork company in 1973, when she was eighteen. The original plan of the organization was to transfer my mother to the beef company, but her father used some connections to change her destiny, and she became a pork seller. At that time, almost everyone — except for Muslims who ate beef — loved pork. The Germans were proud of their pork knuckle and schnitzel, which we consider very childish. There were a hundred ways to prepare a pork dish in China. We were the country that paid attention to superb cuisine. We invented chopsticks more than three thousand years ago. As for when the knife and fork were invented, and when westerners actually used them, I wasn't sure. I felt that using them was scary. They could be weapons.

In the 1970s, people needed vouchers to buy everything including daily necessities: oil, salt, sauce, vinegar, TVs, bicycles, radios, clothing and the like. The most valuable voucher was the pork voucher. If you had it, congratulations, you could eat pork. Which part of the pork, and the quality of meat, however, was not guaranteed. You needed to get along well with my mother. A voucher could only buy a fixed weight of meat. As to the included fat or bones, that was all decided by my powerful mother. It was very hard work. From Monday to Friday, my mother had to get up earlier than the cock. She always arrived at the company around five thirty a.m. to prepare the meat. Business hours were six a.m. to ten a.m. Before she entered the company, people were already lined up outside.

The pork company was about eighty square metres, including a cold storage room, a manager's office around thirty square metres, and two open windows for selling pork, one large and one small. The large one could hold two pork sellers, and the small one could only hold my mother, who was one hundred and fifty-eight cm tall and weighed seventy-nine kilograms.

My mother wore rain boots and a waterproof butcher's apron when she got ready to sell. In front of her was a concrete table three metres long, two metres wide and one metre high. On it, next to a couple of machetes, sat a round, wooden cutting board, almost half my mother's weight. It came from a tree that had existed on earth for at least ten thousand years. The rest of the room was full of different parts of the pig. The three pork sellers were all women. I asked my mother, "Why?"

She returned, "Why not?" There was no reason why! She told me the rice shop and vegetable shop next door both had all female sellers too. This was the rule!

Curly's mother was a seller in the vegetable shop and his aunt was a seller in the rice shop. There was a degree of solidarity and sisterhood amongst them. They often gossiped together about boring things. But I didn't know Curly until I was eleven years old.

When Curly was ten, a big thing happened. The whole family was enraged with Curly's father who wanted to send Curly to sports school but had no idea why. He couldn't convince his family, because he didn't know sports at all.

When I was sent to the sports school, it was quite a different affair, not as complicated. My father made the decision by himself. My mother silently protested and refused to cook for one day. Suddenly, she asked my father why he should send me to the sports school when even the poor carpenter downstairs wouldn't send his son to sports school. My father's answer was full of wisdom.

"The body is the capital of the revolution."

My mother didn't understand how I was the revolution or what the revolution was for. Her big eyes full of anger glared at my father. My father pretended not to see and continued to drink fifty-two percent liquor. He was always very calm, and always uninterested in explaining anything.

Curly's father did not have authority like my father. Their family adhered to democratic centralism. His father failed to convince all family members of his idea. During that time, the family could have cut the atmosphere with a knife. Curly's aunt was the only calm person.

One day, her memory brought her to my mother's workplace.

"Lynn!" Curly's aunt started calling my mother's name ten metres away. "Is your son in sports school?"

"Just went for a year," my mother yelled while loudly chopping the pork.

Curly's aunt breathed a sigh of relief and asked, "What part of the pork is better today?"

"The ribs are very good," my mother cut the cleaver into the chopping block. "You wait for me."

The customers in front of Curly's aunt were all ignored by my mother. She just turned away. After two minutes, she returned with a rib and said, "You take this piece."

"How much is it?" Curly's aunt asked.

"Fifteen Yuan," my mother cut the rib into small pieces. "This piece was originally reserved for my husband's mother."

"This is a nice rib..." some of the customers said with envious eyes.

"Thank you very much!" Curly's aunt smiled like a flower. "You are busy. I won't take up more of your time. Bye!"

The next day, Curly's grandparents came to the pork company.

"Lynn!" Curly's grandma waved enthusiastically.

"Oh, hello!" my mother said with a smile. "Your daughter was just here yesterday. What do you want to buy today?"

"We won't buy meat today," Curly's grandpa's eyes laughed

into a line. He asked, “Is your son in sports school?”

“He’s been there for a year,” my mother blew her hair out of her face. “What happened? Yesterday, your daughter asked the same question.”

“All good!” Curly’s grandpa kept his eyes in a line.

Curly’s grandma said, “My son wants to send my grandson to the sports school. My daughter told us that your son is also in the sports school. We have nothing to do at home. We just wanted to come over and have a chat! Continue your work, and thanks for your time. Bye!”

Day three.

Curly’s mother’s voice echoed from afar.

“Dear Lynn!”

“Hi Sissi!” my mother stood on her tiptoes and lifted her neck, looking over the head of a customer.

Sissi wiggled her hips like a penguin. She pushed past the customer and came up to my mother.

“Lynn, is your son in sports school? Which sport? Which coach? Is it hard to train? You can’t imagine the war at home. My husband is as stubborn as a stupid mule. Even if we killed him, his ghost would insist on sending our son to the sports school. We fight every day, from dawn till dusk. I won’t let him sleep in our bed. I make him sleep on the sofa.” Sissi’s eyebrows were dancing while she talked.

“What are you arguing about?” my mother asked. “My son has been gone for a year and he is still in one piece.”

“Really?” Sissi’s eyes widened with a smile “That’s really awesome.”

“Does your son like sports?” my mother asked.

“You cannot imagine,” Sissi swallowed saliva. “My son can’t stay still for a minute. How about your son? My son—”

"My son is OK, but—"

"OK, your son is definitely not like my son," Sissi chipped in. "I really can't figure it out. My son never took one step in a normal way. Every day, I tell you. Every minute of every day, running around here and there nonstop. Within one month, a pair of shoes are worn out. You don't know how many shoes I've bought for him." Sissi let out a sigh.

"Sports school distributes shoes," my mother said.

"Really? Marvellous! The coach said that there is also a training fee."

"What? Training fee?" my mother scoffed. "I've never heard about that! My son must be a little criminal."

"No, no, no, your son wouldn't lie," Sissi said. "I'm sure the coach was bragging because he wants us to do sports."

"You don't know the little bastard. He often steals his father's money."

"That's not good. You should beat him," Sissi said. "How much pocket money do you give him?"

"Three Yuan a day."

"What? That is too little," Sissi said. "We only give my son five Yuan a day because my parents-in-law also give money to my son. How old is your son?"

"Eleven years old."

"Oh, that's right, one year older than mine," Sissi said. "Lynn, you gave him too little money. No wonder he stole from his father."

"My parents-in-law never give pocket money to my son," my mother complained. "Even though my parents occasionally give him some."

"That's different," Sissi said. "You shouldn't compare it to me. They only have one grandson."

"That makes sense," my mother said. "They have two grandsons."

"You see," Sissi looked at her watch. "Oh my god, I have been talking with you for so long that I must have delayed your business!"

"It doesn't matter," my mother said. "The pork leg is good today. Do you want some?"

"Not today, thank you. I have to go back to work. See you!"

Day Four.

Curly's father dressed neatly and queued up at the pork company. After thirty minutes, he made his way to the front and pushed up his glasses.

My mother found him. "Oh Frank," she said. "How are you? What do you want to buy?"

"Hello Lynn, long time no see. I am fine, thank you. And you?"

"Do you want to buy something or not!" someone shouted from the crowd.

"Oh sorry!" Frank stood aside and asked my mother, "Will I interrupt your work here?"

"Not at all!" my mother said. "You came to ask about the sports school, right?" my mother finished her question and yelled to the customer: "What do you want!"

"What event does your son practice at the sports school?" Frank asked.

"High jump or long jump, I'm not sure," answered my mother, and then she shouted at the customer, "Don't touch the meat! If you want it, just take it!"

"What? Can't I check it?" the customer said. "Can you cut the fat meat away?"

"No way! If I cut the fat, who will buy it?" my mother said.

"If you don't want the meat, please move away. Don't interrupt my work."

"The name of the coach is Tom?" Frank asked.

"It seems to be 'Tom' or 'Tim'. I can't remember it very clearly." My mother shouted again, "Don't touch the meat! Do you hear me!"

"OK, OK, what's with the attitude?" The customer pointed at the meat, "This piece."

My mother threw the meat on the scale.

"Could you cut it into eight pieces for me?" the customer asked.

"Twenty-two, point eighty-six Yuan," my mother said. "I have no time. Please take it home and cut it yourself."

"It should be the same coach," Frank continued. "So, destiny can tie the two boys together. Bring your son over one day. I've never seen the little one before. Let the two boys get to know each other and play together in the future. I will take my leave. Goodbye Lynn!"

"Twenty-two Yuan," the customer said.

"Please take care, Frank, bye!" My mother's voice was very polite until Frank walked away and she yelled, "This is a state-operated butcher shop, not a private butcher shop! If you want a discount, don't come here!"

CHAPTER III

When I entered the sports school, my eyes were full of people running and jumping. My blood began to boil. I had the feeling of finding home, like a zoo monkey returning to the Amazon. But in my ear, I heard people shouting out strange codes, none of which were people's names: "Bronze pot," "Doorbell," "Pony" and others.

Before the sports school, I went to the normal primary school. There were about fifty students in one class and ten classes in one grade. I was in the top ten students in my grade. My head teacher did not clearly understand why my father sent me to the sports school. He insisted on talking to my father. I didn't know what they talked about. But when I left, my head teacher wished for me not to become a strong bodied, but a simple-minded person. So, when I heard those strange code names, I remembered the head teacher's warning. As I looked deeper, though, I realized that I was wrong. All the calls were nicknames. They were the crystallization of blood and wisdom.

"Pony" was an athlete on the sprint team. He ran very fast, and his movement was elegant like a horse. So, his nickname was Pony. "Bronze Pot" was an athlete on the throwing team. He did shot put. His figure was like a teapot, but he wasn't as fragile as a teapot. He could fight with ten athletes at the same time. He was an unbreakable teapot. "Doorbell" was an athlete on the long jump team. One day, while Bronze Pot and his teammates were shot put training, Doorbell was walking by and reading a

Japanese comic book. He didn't realize he was in the danger zone. A two-kilogram shot put hit him in the head and knocked him down. The coach took him to the hospital on a tricycle. Everyone thought that if he survived, he would be handicapped. But we were wrong. When he came back from his injury, he looked the same as before. Only, his head was missing some hair. Someone put a ping-pong ball on his scar. It looked like a bird's nest, so people tried to call him "Nest". Doorbell didn't mind the nickname, but when people called him "Nest", most of them also touched the round scar. This action always irritated him. He was shouting or beating the people who touched his scar. Once, he growled at someone, "Snotty bastard! This is not a doorbell. Don't press it!"

My nickname was "Egghead", a name granted to me because I was scrawny with a big head. Only the teacher of the general knowledge course called me by my actual name.

Sports school was no different from an ordinary school in appearance. There was a small building for the general knowledge course. Monday to Friday, rainy days exempted, the Five-Star Red Flag rose at eight a.m. and the national anthem played. Most of the general knowledge teachers and sports students would salute and sing the national anthem on the playground. None of the sports coaches would be there. They only showed up after two p.m., when we finished the general knowledge courses, or if there were some serious fight, and the school needed them to intervene.

Before the athletes went to training, they had to suffer through mathematics, physics, chemistry, Chinese, English, biology, geography, history, politics, health and music lessons. The athletes who performed well on the field would sleep during class, read comic books, listen to pop song, pass notes, eat and drink. The performance of the rest of the athletes was more random. Someone caught a stray cat. Some gambled with cards, and the loser would pay money, owe snacks or lunch, get slapped… They could bet on anything. One person smoked. Another played with insects. Most of the older male athletes were molesting female athletes or female athletes were flirting with male athletes.

There were nine grades in the school, from the fourth grade of primary school to the third grade of high school. There was only one class per grade. The students ranged from ten to eighteen years old, with about two hundred athletes selected from a region with a population of three million inhabitants.

The criteria for selecting athletes, was first their height, and second their parents' heights. The average height of my parents was one hundred and sixty-five centimetres. Ironically, I entered the high jump team.

My coach didn't want me at first, I was not tall or strong and I looked like an egghead. There was a girl who tested with me that year. She was half a head taller than me. The coach wanted her, and her parents disagreed. My coach still had an enrolment quota he had to fulfil, or he would get a deduction from his salary. He asked me some questions, such as the work of my parents, and my learning situation. He thought that I was a well-behaved child who would not cause trouble for him.

Then, just one day after my first anniversary of sports school survival, my mother told me very happily that I would have a little friend. I was indifferent. My heart already felt ninety-nine years old, too old to make new friends. My mother was so excited, as though she had made a good friend. I didn't want to abuse her kindness and said, "Let me think about it."

My mother didn't give a shit about my thoughts. I don't

know why adults always ignore their kids' thoughts. They always think their choices are best. They don't give you any chance to show your opinion. Even when you are seventy years old, if your father is still around, he would treat you like a child and never consider your feelings.

In my memory as an eleven-year-old, with the exception of the Spring Festival, my parents never took me to visit anyone. If I found a few red wrapped candies, it meant someone got married. If I saw an egg in a red shell, it meant that a baby was born. If I had noodles in a red bowl, it meant someone had a birthday. Because city housing was allocated by the government during the Planned Economy Period, everyone's houses were almost all the same size: thirty square metres including a kitchen, bathroom, bedroom and balcony for a family of three. If you were lucky enough to have twins, and you were a family of four, you would get forty square metres. There wasn't any space for guests, so no one was interested in hosting one another. The relationships between neighbours and relatives were still very good, though. That's why it was unprecedented for my parents to visit someone on a summer evening, getting dressed up and carrying fruit.

I followed my parents from home and walked three hundred metres west. It took six minutes until we found the building in the moonlight. We touched the stair railing, climbed three floors and rang the doorbell of the second apartment. There came a soft beam of light accompanied by a sharp voice through the dark corridor.

"Finally, here you are!" Sissi said with her crow's feet smiling at me. "Oh, this is little Flynn. So cute."

"Just... One more floor... Than my apartment... Makes me... Out of breath... Sissi," my mother said with difficulty.

"Please come in," said Frank. He was wearing a white

collared short-sleeved shirt, standing behind Sissi with a smile.

My mother was entangled with Sissi and blocking the entrance.

"I told you again and again! Don't buy anything." Sissi took my mother's hand. "Leave it beside the door. Take it home later."

"Don't badger me," my mother shook the plastic bag in her hand. "There's a bunch of bananas inside. I went out of my way to ask your mother-in-law."

Sissi took the plastic bag and put it on the ground and said, "Flynn also likes to eat bananas. Take it back when you go back. Otherwise, I won't be happy."

"Don't be silly!" My mother took back the plastic bag and pointed at me. "If he wants it, I'll buy it tomorrow."

Frank reached out, took the plastic bag from my mother, and put it on the table. He expressed his thanks and told my mother she didn't need to buy anything next time, and to make herself at home.

Sissi put three pairs of slippers in front of us and told us to come in quickly.

"Son," called Frank. "Get up! Here they come... Your uncle, aunty and brother."

Sissi stared at Frank and said, "Your son still has a fever."

"What?" my mother asked. "The kid has a fever? Why did you let him get up?"

"That's right!" Sissi showed the whites of her eyes to Frank. "He is the most ridiculous man."

"Who is ridiculous? You or me?" Frank took a step back and pointed to Sissi, then to the bedroom. "Guests come to visit, and your son is impolite in bed."

"There are three chairs and a double sofa in the bedroom, it is already full. Your son has no seat," Sissi said.

“Take this!” Frank took a small stool from the kitchen.

“Thank God for your quick thinking!” Sissi raised her eyebrows dismissively. “Perfect for you!”

“Never mind the stool,” my father took a pack of cigarettes from his shirt pocket and held one out to Frank. “Let my son sit on the stool.”

I glanced sideways at my father. My father raised his hand and pretended to beat me. I took a step back as a physiological reflex and just brushed against my mother. She was sweating and very concerned about being touched. She pushed me away complaining. My father’s forehand slapped my face without any notice.

“What the fuck!” I was covering the left side of my face and as my voice dropped, I heard another clear sound from my father’s backhand slap. The beaten face was still my face, only it was the right side now, in order to maintain a balance for violent aesthetics.

If given the chance, my father could have become a tennis star with his forehand and backhand attacks. It was impossible to defend effectively.

At that time, though, I was still only eleven years old. So, I couldn’t control my emotions very well. My mother said that I deserved it. As my parents, they certainly had the right to decide if I should be beaten or not. Sometimes I agreed; sometimes I was just confused. For example, if I was angry, I would blurt out that my mother was a pig. Under this circumstance, I would expect to be beaten, and I wouldn’t cry or scream.

In this moment, however, my tears and the noise I let out were automatic. My father felt uncomfortable but my mother’s reaction boosted his morale. Sissi’s reaction was great, though. She pulled me behind her back. Frank took out his lighter and lit my father's cigarette.

"Smoke in the kitchen," Sissi said.

Frank bent his arm round my father's shoulder and they went into the kitchen.

"Let's go into the room." Sissi pushed me forward three steps.

A boy was lying on the queen size bed with his chin in his hands. He looked at me like I was an alien. The bed occupied forty percent of the bedroom. I looked at him and shivered. The whole summer that I was training under the sun, I thought I was becoming dark. But compared to him, I looked like Snow White.

Sissi invited me to sit on the sofa with her. I was happy to take her up on her kindness, but in the end, I still sat on the small stool. Although Curly was in bed all night, an empty loyal chair was waiting for him from the beginning to the end.

The adults spent the whole evening discussing whether or not there was water to drink at the sports school and whether or not pocket money would be misused. Would the boys be hungry and have a good meal? No one looked forward to the future. Even college they dared not think about. The world champion was someone they hadn't even heard of, and the complex environment of the sports school was even more unimaginable.

Before we left, Frank delivered a short speech. He said that Curly and I were to be good brothers who take care of each other. His left hand held my right hand, and his right hand held Curly's left hand, like a boxing referee. But this was somewhat different. He didn't raise anyone's hand and declare who was the winner. Instead, he put our two little hands together.

I feel a little shy revealing this kind of ceremony.

CHAPTER IV

The sports school had summer holidays like ordinary schools, but only for the general knowledge course teachers. Coaches and athletes didn't get a vacation, especially the high jump coach. Other sports team had weekends off. The high jump team didn't have a single holiday, no weekends, no Children's Day, no Women's Day, no Labour Day, not even the National Holiday. There were three hundred and sixty-five days in a year. The high jump team only received three days off during the Spring Festival, because our coach was a fan of the Soviet novel, *How the Steel Was Tempered*. In front of him, we called him Coach Tom, behind his back, we called him "Iron Ox".

At the beginning of the new term in September, I begged my mother to call Iron Ox and to tell him that I had diarrhoea so I needed sick leave for two days. The truth was that I had to finish my summer homework. My head teacher was very fussy about such things. I was not afraid of him at all, but he would report my situation to Iron Ox like a sissy. And then, I would be terminated.

Once, the fiercest man on our team had a serious fight in class. He destroyed the teacher's podium. His nickname was "Garlic". After being notified of the damage, the head teacher rushed into the classroom like a fire fighter. He scanned the scene in one second. Then, he turned away without hesitation, went back to the office and made a phone call.

The head teacher hung up the phone and went to the crosswalk at the school gate. His eyes were fixated on the path that looked like the bowel of a sheep. He was crooning a Beijing Opera. The longer the noise came out of his mouth, the happier he became. Then he saw a man entering his field of vision. A man with a straight figure like a pine tree; a man who walked fast and vigorously like the wind; a man who had a ruddy complexion, black hair like a steel needle, and eyes blazing like torches. The head teacher reached his climax. He stretched out his neck, waved his hands, then whooped, "Dear Coach Tom!"

Iron Ox kept his chin up and chest out. The head teacher was leading the way like a donkey in a lion's path.

After the fight, the mess was everywhere in the class. Broom, mop, eraser, chalk — all was in wild disorder. The head teacher approached the class with vigorous strides, popped his head in and looked about.

"Who is looking for trouble?" Garlic was shouting and throwing a blackboard eraser. The head teacher made a magnificent turn and successfully dodged the attack.

"Me!" Iron Ox's voice was like surround sound stereo. The whole building trembled. He went into the classroom and pointed to Garlic

"You piece of shit!" Garlic was staring at the head teacher. "Snitch! You just wait and see."

"See what?" Iron Ox sprinted up, and knocked the top of Garlic's head. "How dare you!"

Garlic gasped in pain. He whipped a mirror out of his pocket, quickly tidied up his hairstyle and shouted forward to the head teacher, "You're dead! You hear me? You're dead!"

"I'd like to see who's dead," Iron Ox wanted to use his unique skill again. Garlic instinctively covered his head with both arms, bent his waist, and raised one leg high, knee bent, until his hip was at a ninety-degree angle. It almost looked like he was in an airplane brace position during a turbulent flight. So, after his perfect defence, he only got a kick in the ass.

Garlic was the oldest and most powerful athlete on our team. He could do twenty dips on the parallel in a row. But Iron Ox was more powerful than Garlic. When he was a soldier, he had to chat with his comrades while he did dips on the bars, otherwise, he would fall asleep. Everyone had heard the story, but no one questioned it. Until I showed up. I didn't believe in Iron Ox's bullshit.

Iron Ox nodded with great satisfaction. He jumped on the parallel bars with ease, and said with a smile, "Count it for me."

"One, two, three… Fourteen, fifteen… Twenty-eight…" we counted in unison.

"See? Can I chat with you? How many?" Iron Ox asked.

"Thirty-two… Forty-eight…" The voices of the crowd grew louder and louder.

"Can you all see? Fifty, piece of cake." Iron Ox's nose was blowing, and he didn't want to breathe with his mouth. He asked, "Who else doubts? Who else is unwilling to surrender?"

For the next week, his arm seemed to be short of oil and his movements were not very coordinated.

CHAPTER V

The first of September. A new term, new school, new teacher, new classmates, new schoolbag, new stationery, new clothes, new trousers, new shoes, new socks… Curly was a newcomer through and through. The anticipation and excitement of the unknown environment woke him up earlier than the alarm clock. He went into the bathroom and rode on the toilet like someone riding a horse. His mother hated men who spray their urine everywhere. When he finished urinating, the alarm clock rang.

"Wake up your son, Frank," Sissi's voice came from the kitchen.

Frank walked out of the bedroom with sleepy eyes. Sissi held the spatula and wanted to walk into the bedroom. They were blocked at the door of the toilet.

"So smelly," Sissi opened the bathroom door.

"What are you watching?" Curly changed his posture, and prepared to squeeze a shit. "Close the door!"

"Who wants to see you?" Sissi closed the door condescendingly. "Don't forget to flush the toilet and wash your hands!"

"So annoying!" Curly said.

"My kindness came to no good," Sissi soliloquized.

"You're really annoying!" Frank said. "The bathroom door was closed. Why would you open it?"

"It was obvious that someone was inside," Curly yelled.

"Shut up, you two," Sissi said. "Eat your breakfast and leave me alone."

After breakfast, as soon as Curly left home, he began to run. At that time, I was sitting aside the flowerbed, chin in hands, facing his building. Almost at the same time I saw Curly and heard Sissi's voice.

"Flynn, why don't you come up?" Sissi asked.

"Dad, here he comes!" Curly said and ran away.

"Good morning, Flynn. Have you had breakfast?" Frank came towards me with a bag of milk and steamed buns.

"Good morning, I… I have eaten," I stammered and just wanted to tell a white lie. I was still unfamiliar with them and my mother always taught me not to take advantage of others.

"Give him breakfast," Sissi called out. Her voice was floating in the air. "He definitely hasn't had breakfast yet, I know."

I accepted the breakfast passively; my heart was not very comfortable. Frank asked me to follow him, and I followed him. He asked me to eat steamed buns, and I ate steamed buns. He asked me to drink milk, so I drank milk. He told me to eat slowly. But that was the only instruction I didn't follow. I finished breakfast in two minutes. My stomach felt good and I saw Curly standing in front of a car.

Frank was the driver for the electric company. He didn't drive an electrician's yellow emergency repair van. He drove for the leaders. Because the leaders were always busy until late at night, and many people wanted to invite them for dinner and drinks, the leaders could not wake up earlier than the students. So, Frank had the chance to use the car for private purposes.

I followed Curly's ass and sat very seriously in the car, like frozen meat. My instincts didn't kick in, they just made me feel nervous. Curly was playing with a seatbelt fast, then slowly, then gently, then fiercely. I didn't know what he was doing. I also didn't know it was a safety belt until Frank said, "Stop playing with the safety belt." I still didn't know what a safety belt was for because no one used them, I mean even the driver.

Frank started the engine and the cool air blew out. He turned the steering wheel and talked about my mother's job, the weather, the food in the school, about how he would pick us up after school. I was still in frozen mode, so I couldn't talk to him. He asked me if I had ever been in a jeep. I shook my head.

"He has never been in a jeep," Curly answered the question for me and informed me of the make. "TOYOTA Land Cruiser imports from Japan."

"This is by far the best jeep in Shanghai," Frank said.

"It's also the most expensive car," Curly said. "Worth ten thousand dollars."

"Don't talk nonsense," Frank said. "Do you know how much ten thousand dollars is?"

"One million dollars," Curly continued. "Ninety-nine thousand nine hundred and ninety-nine dollars."

If you've been with Curly for a long time, you would find that he often entered his own world. But at that moment, I thought his math was good.

Frank wanted to drive to the school gate, but his experience told him that narrow alleys were hard to enter, and nearly impossible to get out. The slum in front of him had no way of getting cars through. Frank looked for a place to park for ten minutes. He wanted to walk in with us. The more he tried, the more difficult it became. His car obstructed the busy morning of the slum. The people were very unfriendly and shouted at him to go away. Some man insulted him saying he was a dick to drive the car in there. The women were more polite, calling him a freak, fool or psycho. But no one dared to touch the car or spit on it.

I followed Curly and jumped out of the car quickly. Frank honked the horn and left. Someone cursed his horn; Someone spit on the ground. I felt a little nervous. The situation seemed quite inconsequential to Curly. He kicked away a small stone by the side of the road.

"Where is the school?" Curly asked.

"There," I said, pointing to a bare flagpole. "Not far from us."

"Let's run!" Curly counted down, "Three, two…"

My reaction was very fast and by the time Curly arrived at the count of one, his voice was already behind me. He chased me and said I cheated. Soon, he ran ahead of me and laughed at me, "You are too slow!"

He ran to the school gate, took out the red scarf from his schoolbag and put it around his neck. I was a second behind him.

"What are you doing?" I asked.

"I am a member of the Young Pioneers of China," Curly said.

The sight reminded me of a day one year before. My father rode a bicycle and took me to the school gate. I wore a brand-new red scarf and went into the school. I performed the young pioneers' ritual to all the teachers when I met them. I even greeted some tall guys that I thought were teachers. Later, I found out that nobody wore red scarves. No teacher cared about that. It took me one week to understand why. It was too late when I finally gave up the red scarf. People already knew I was a new fish.

"So what?" I came back to the present. "We all know that the red scarf is the tip of the iceberg of our duty to the five-star red flag, dyed by the blood of martyrs."

"We can't enter school without a red scarf," Curly said.

"No need here," I said. "Take it off."

Curly did not hesitate to take off the red scarf. His cooperation saved me a lot of saliva.

"Come with me," I said.

"I don't want to pee." Curly followed me until he reached the toilet.

"Shut up and come in." My face was beyond question. I opened the door and pulled Curly into the stall.

"How much money do you have?" I asked.

"What do you want?"

"Shut up and tell me."

"Ten Yuan." Curly's face was taut and terrified.

"Give it all to me." I demanded.

"Why?" Curly tilted his neck and stared at me.

"I will keep it safe for you."

"Don't worry," Curly said. "I have already hidden my money in my shoes."

"It was quite clever of you to think that way," I nodded. "But still, you're too young, too naive."

"Where did you hide your money?" Curly didn't believe there was anywhere better.

"I don't have to hide my money," I said. "I don't have time to explain the problem to you. You will understand it sooner or later."

I saw the question mark on Curly's face. I didn't have to hide my money because I had to pay protection money. I didn't think I had the ability to explain the problem in such a short time. I heard someone come in. I lowered my voice and asked Curly to give me the money. I explained if I hijacked his money, he could tell his mother, and his mother would tell my mother, and my mother would tell my father, and my father would hang me up like a dried salted fish.

Curly liked the prospect of me hanging up like a fish. He took off his left shoe, took out the insole, and took out a bill. I grabbed the money and put in my pocket.

I guided Curly to his classroom — Grade Five. I had been promoted to Grade Six. The Grade Five students were coming from Grade Four. There wasn't an age restriction for when you could start training. So usually, the younger you started, the better. Grade politics in sports schools was very strict. The younger grade had to respect the older grade, because older grades' bodies were stronger. For example, like in a zoo, Grade Five's zoo class, had a rabbit, wolf, elephant and tiger. Grade Six's zoo class, also had a rabbit, wolf, elephant and tiger. The younger rabbit usually could not defeat the older rabbit. A younger wolf absolutely could bite an older rabbit, even if the older rabbit was one hundred years old. But the younger wolf dared not touch the older rabbit, because the older wolf would protect the older rabbit. The flesh cannot let the younger take advantage, maintaining the balance of ecosystem.

If Curly had started in the fourth grade, the initial grade in the sports school, I would not take him to his class because Grade Four was full of fresh meat — no one knew who I was — and they hadn't been polluted yet. Starting in the fifth grade was the worst thing for Curly. After a year of pollution, most fresh meat had become smoked bacon. What's more, they would wait for their past selves. Sometimes, there would be fresh meat put into the fifth grade, like me last year. I was an additional reward who was under the same roof as the smoked bacon. I was isolated; however, I was lucky, and I didn't suffer much. After a cultural examination, I was appointed to be the president of the class by the head teacher. Grade Five students wouldn't dare defy teachers yet. In my class, the fiercer a man was, the worse his grades were.

They needed to copy my homework. I made some good friendships. Although the sports school had cultural homework, it was so simple that even the dimwits could do it. In fact, they were not very stupid, just unwilling.

Doorbell was the last person to do his homework, and he was the first person who failed to move up to the next grade in the history of the sports school. I had a bad relationship with him. In one fight, he gave me a panda eye. From then on, I avoided physical conflict with him. It's not because I was timid, because Doorbell's penis grew hairs and mine didn't. *If you understand this, you understand it. If you don't, I'll explain later.* Let me go back to, "I guided Curly to his classroom."

There were two girl teammates in the same class with Curly. One was Kitty, another one was Fox Eye.

"What the hell are you doing here, Egghead," Fox Eye asked.

"You, stink fox fart, get out of my face and don't pollute my eyes," I said. "And by the way, do me a favour. Shave your beard, please."

"Don't bullshit with him," Kitty jumped out. "His mouth is like a toilet."

I exhaled at Curly and asked, "Is my breath that bad?"

Curly was not very cooperative and avoided my face.

"You see? Your mouth really stinks like a rotten egg," said Fox Eye.

"That's because you have to sit on it whenever you use it and don't clean it." I put my arm around Curly's shoulder. "Unlike us. We are usually standing up."

"I don't know what he's talking about," Kitty said.

"Hi man, what's your name? Which team are you on?" Fox Eye asked Curly.

"He is my brother," I said. "Take care of him."

Curly greeted and introduced himself.

"Seems like a nice guy," Kitty said, then warned, "Don't get too close to Egghead."

"Who is Egghead?" Curly asked.

"Let go of your hand. Don't pretend to be familiar." Fox Eye pulled me away from Curly.

"That's the way Egghead is. He likes to pretend to be a big brother," Kitty said.

"Very good!" I said and held out my hand.

Kitty and Fox Eye were very reluctant to give one Yuan each for protection.

"Egghead, you seem to be in the wrong class." Doorbell twitched his shoulders and approached me with his sneer.

"It's none of your business," I said.

"Sorry, monitor!" Doorbell gave me a phony salute and patted his forehead. "Goddamn, I forgot. You are not the president of my class."

I rolled my eyes heavenward in disgust. Pretending to be severe, I gave Kitty a look that meant taking care of Curly.

"Don't worry!" Doorbell came up and put his arm around Curly's neck. "I'll take care of him."

"Let him go, failure!" I said.

Curly broke free of Doorbell's arm and came to my side. I put my arm around Curly's shoulder. Curly was very cooperative now and put his arm around my shoulder. We looked like two Rugby players. Doorbell shrugged us off and turned his lecherous eyes to Kitty.

"Get the hell out of here," Fox Eye said. "Ugly pervert!"

"Who are you talking about?" Doorbell grabbed Fox Eye's ponytail.

"Let her go, you piece of shit!" I said.

"OK," Doorbell was loosening his grip. "Good men don't fight women." He came at me and pushed my chest. "How about you? Let's have a duel."

"If you like to fight so much, go to the boxing team," I said. "I don't want to touch low-IQ creatures."

I have such a bitchy tongue, sometimes; it really hurts. Some people even want to kill me.

Doorbell grabbed my clothes and shook me. More and more people came to watch, most of them anxious to see the world in disorder. They shouted one thing after another, encouraging us to fight. I had no reaction, poker-faced. I wouldn't fulfil their stupid wishes.

"Leave him alone, Doorbell!" someone shouted. I could tell it was Garlic, one of my protectors.

"Doorbell thought his body grew well," I said.

"Really?" Garlic pointed at Doorbell's nose. "Take off your pants. Show me. How many hairs do you have?"

"Not as many as you," Doorbell said.

"What?" Garlic slapped Doorbell on the top of his head. "Who do you think you are talking to?"

"Me!" Bronze Pot joined the party.

"What's the matter with you?" Garlic looked at Bronze Pot and kept his finger pointed at Doorbell. "He beat my teammate."

"I didn't!" Doorbell said.

"You see," Bronze Pot started. "I am upholding justice."

"Did you eat too much?" Garlic asked. "Who is he to you?"

Doorbell didn't know it was Bronze Pot who hit his head with the shotput and almost killed him. But Bronze Pot knew and felt very bad about it, although it wasn't his fault.

"He is nobody to me," Bronze Pot said with steady eyes. "I

like to uphold justice. Do you want to go against me? Are you hairy enough to challenge me?"

"Don't bullshit me!" Garlic said. "If you like to uphold justice, I'll jump off the building immediately."

"You can jump now," Bronze Pot said. "Climb to the roof to jump. It's only three floors. You won't die."

I was tired of their conversation. The bell for class rang just in time. I told Curly to wait for me to have lunch together.

At noon, the school was boiling. Most male athletes and a few female athletes banged their steel bowls with their spoons or chopsticks. Someone banged the wall; Someone banged the stair handrail; Someone banged someone's head. Imitated animal sounds were everywhere. Wolf howls were the most popular, and then dog barks, tiger roars, happy crow caw, duck quacks and some insect sounds you could almost not hear. The Amazon Forest probably sounds like that.

On the way to the canteen, I pointed at the tall, short, wide and narrow athletes, introduced their nicknames to Curly and explained how they got their nicknames. At that time, my hunch was that Curly would get a nickname like "Chimpanzee" or something about being black.

At the entrance of the canteen, we met Iron Ox. He was waiting to give new comers meal tickets. I also needed meal tickets, but Iron Ox ignored me and pushed Curly to go for lunch first. What I was worried about finally happened. I took my note from my pocket, about my diarrhoea. Not only had I asked my mother to call for sick leave, I also had her write a note.

"Diarrhoea, very good. Don't eat lunch. It's a waste," Iron Ox said.

"I am fine now." I squeezed a flattering smile.

"What are you waiting for?" Iron Ox asked Curly.

"Me!" I explained, and Curly gave a nod of agreement.

Iron Ox was not surprised at all that I was with Curly. He raised his arm and prepared to knock me on the head. I looked at him very sincerely and didn't shrink my neck. He changed his gesture, yanked my ear and warned me not to bully my new teammate.

"Is that clear?" Iron Ox asked.

"Couldn't be clearer!" My ear was pulled like a trombone.

The food was not bad on the first day: fried pork, greens, sausage tomato soup and unlimited rice. We sat with Kitty and Fox Eye.

"Look at the meat in her bowl," I said. "That's steak."

"Stop daydreaming, Egghead!" Kitty said.

I told Curly that Kitty was Hui nationality, so she ate beef every day. She couldn't eat pork. Her religion didn't allow it, because their ancestor was hunted down by bad men and fell off a cliff. A super big pig caught him like a cushion, so they worship pigs and it's forbidden to eat them.

"Nonsense!" Kitty said. "It's just because pigs are dirty."

"Dirty how?" I asked.

"I don't want to talk to you about it," Kitty said.

"Because you only eat beef, you're already possessed by cow," I said. "You run slower than a cow, jump lower than a cow... Your physical strength is like a cow."

"Don't forget that she ran faster than you, so you are slower than a cow," Fox Eye said.

"If you keep silent, no one thinks you're dumb," I said. "Please, do me a favour, put your face in your bowl."

Fox Eye blew a gust of wind through her nostrils.

"You are slower than her?" Curly asked.

"What?" I asked. "You think you can win against her?"

Curly shook his head with a sneer.

For the rest of lunch time, I became the object of ridicule and scorn.

After lunch, I wanted to check if Curly could beat Kitty in a race or not. I walked into the toilet naturally, and Curly followed me. I took off my pants naturally, and Curly followed me. I peeked at his penis, it looked like a peanut.

"What are you looking at?" Curly found my greedy eyes were on his private parts. He turned his back toward me and twisted his head around to try and see my privates.

"Please feel free to look around," I said naturally. "You and I are the same level, nothing special."

"What do you mean by that?" Curly zipped his trousers up.

We left the toilet and wandered on the playground. I started to explain body science.

"Could a bird fly when it comes out of its shell?" I asked.

"I don't know."

"What? You don't know? For God's sake, please don't tease me," I said. "This is a very serious topic."

Curly tried to think hard and replied, "Baby birds are in the nest. The mother bird catches insects for them to eat."

"That means they can't fly," I said. "They have to wait until their feathers grow."

"So what?" Curly asked.

I felt like that I was playing the piano to a hippo. Curly had no idea about puberty. However, he would be inspired later on. Physical examination and physical fitness tests were held in the afternoon on the first day of sport school. The anniversary of my first day at the sports school was just around the corner. That afternoon, the coach gave me a form. The form was for measurements and test results. Things like standing height, sitting height, higher limb length, thigh length, calf length, ankle width, arm span, weight, bone age, reaction speed test, lung capacity, haemoconcentration, one-minute sit-ups, standing long jump, sixty-metre dash, eight-hundred-metre, long distance race. There was only one unit I didn't quite understand. It was called "Development Degree".

Curly got the same form I had received. He had two questions on the form: one was about haemoconcentration, and the other one about Development Degree. He got his first result after the acupuncture on his ring finger. His blood's number value was fifteen — super good. Mine was twelve, higher than normal people but not stunning. Curly wanted to learn the second result directly. I stopped him and asked him to leave that test for the end before he started his fitness test.

Curly saw some people came out of the "Development Degree" room. Most of them folded the paper. Some people were asking each other for their results. Several people whispered and compared their numbers in the corner. Someone had just written something on the paper themself.

There was only one Development Degree check room, no gender distinction, one person out, one person in. By coincidence, I saw Kitty just come out. I snatched her form quickly when she wasn't looking.

"Woo… Level II! Woo…" Honestly, I was not very sure what I was wooing about. The year before, I was given Level zero. I remember Doorbell was Level I. Garlic was Level III, and the maximum was Level V.

I could guess what the meaning from zero to V was, but I couldn't feel it, because I was zero. Zero meant nothing, like a blank sheet of paper.

"You trash, I ought to bury you alive." Kitty recaptured her form and said, “I will tell coach Tom.”

“Oh no, please don’t!” Although I didn’t do anything excessive, my nervous reflex was to fear Iron Ox. So, I begged her and promised to treat her to ice cream.

Finally, we had to face the test. There was hardly a queue outside the door. Curly had the same feelings that I had last year, like curiosity mixed with anticipation and a little fear. So, I went in first. I pushed through the door. Inside was a woman about my grandma’s age, the same person as last year. Although I had the past year of experience, I was still shy about pulling my pants down in front of her, and she would touch my balls up and down. But I quickly thought of a prank. I yelled when I pulled my pants down.

“What are you yelling for?” the grandmother asked me. “Lift up your testicles.” She didn’t check my balls like she did last year. I felt a little bit confused. I was wondering if testicles were balls. I had never heard of this term.

“You like standing like this, don’t you?”

I thought it was a signal for me to put on my pants.

“Who told you to put on your pants?”

I felt confused again. I didn’t know what I wanted to do or where I could go. The grandmother seemed to think that I was a moron. She drew a circle on my form and asked me to leave.

When I walked out of the room, my prank worked. Curly wanted to know what was happening and the grandma saw there was some one standing outside when the door opened.

“Next one.”

Curly didn’t move one foot.

“Next one.”

“No worries!” I pretended that I was in pain. “I am still in one piece.”

When Curly went in the room, I can hear his nerves from the grandma's voice.

"Pull your pants down... What are you waiting for? Do you want me to invite you for dinner? What's wrong with you? Can you hear me? Do you want me to pull your pants down? Oh my God, who is your coach?"

In a moment, I heard real yelling from Curly and the grandma's complaints. Curly almost cried when he came out of the room. I pretended to care about him and asked him what had happened.

"She touched my balls!" Curly said. I tapped him on the shoulder and took his form to see: the same result as mine.

After the physical fitness test, I found Curly was just as mediocre as me. He did fewer sit-ups than I did; his standing long jump was two centimetres further than mine; his sixty-metre dash was zero point one second faster than me. In the eight-hundred-metre, long distance race, he was a turtle. I was a rabbit.

All athletes on the high jump team handed their completed forms to Iron Ox. He silently counted and said, "Seventeen. One more... Who is missing?"

There were eighteen athletes on our team. I didn't want to introduce them one by one. Most people in my eyes were copy and paste, nothing special.

When we were fully developed, the heights of the male teammates were between one hundred and seventy-eight centimetres and two hundred and three centimetres; female teammates were between one hundred and sixty-eight centimetres and one hundred and eighty-eight centimetres. The tallest and the shortest were in the minority. In the end, I was one hundred and eighty-six centimetres; Curly was one hundred and eighty-nine centimetres; Kitty was one hundred and seventy-three centimetres. Garlic said that he was one hundred and eighty-two centimetres, but the truth was one hundred and seventy-eight centimetres. Male athletes always faked their height higher; some female athlete faked their height lower. Fox Eye's real height was on hundred and eight-three centimetres, but she said her height was one hundred and seventy-six centimetres. When Garlic was standing beside her, both of them insisted that their height was just like that.

At that time, my height was only one hundred and fifty-five centimetres, like a midget. Curly was almost the same. We were not developing, so we didn't know how to appreciate the long-legged beauties all over the playground. Someone began to appreciate it, though. He was Doorbell.

In order to make it easier for athletes to piss during training, next to the playground, there was a small concrete box, two entrances without doors. A thirty-centimetre-wide cement wall divided the space into two parts. The space on the left was the men's toilet and the space on the right was the women's toilet. Along the back wall, there was a nine-metre-long open sewage canal connecting the men's and women's toilets. In the two back corners of the box, there was a water tank with the rope to pull and flush the toilets. The communal river of shit flowed to middle wall and met at the hole beneath it. There were waist-height cement dividers creating stalls. This would satisfy three people simultaneously excreting without seeing each other's struggling faces and smooth buttocks.

Athletes like Doorbell who had simple minds and developing bodies began to have primitive curiosity about the opposite sex. Although it was sports school, coaches forbid puppy love. Doorbell with some others had the same thought. When they heard the sounds from the women's toilet, they heard angels singing. Their blood began to boil; their veins began to swell. They formed a gang. Someone stood at the door as a lookout, to whistle when a coach was coming. If any girl chose the closest cubicle to the men's toilet, this girl squatted down with her back to the wall and there would be a man ready to make his move.

It was not an easy job to spy on girls. Doorbell stood with his legs on either side of the river, back to the partition wall and bent his body forward as much as possible, like a swimmer getting ready to start. And then he stuck his head in the groove. He was facing the hole of shit, pee or fart, no one knew. The blood flew to his head, and turned his face to a pig liver's colour. He was so absorbed that he could not turn away. He saw several insects creeping, but he could not see the beauty he wanted to see.

One prayed that he was invisible; one wanted to make a hole in the wall; one wanted to have a long neck like an ostrich. After all that imagination and hard work, the Devil was touched by their spirit and let them discover the reflection of mirrors. However, God didn't allow it to go too far. They were soon detected, Doorbell and his group were punched and kicked by their coaches.

CHAPTER VI

Curly followed me around for two weeks, and then he started to slack off and become a copycat. There was a saying in China — A good example will be hard to learn, but a bad one will be easy to learn.

When I kicked Pony's ass for fun, Curly took the opportunity to slap it, and Pony punched him back. When I pulled Fox Eye's hair, Curly's hands felt the itch to do the same, and Fox Eye pointed her finger at his nose and warned him. When I charged Kitty one Yuan for protection, he also charged her for his protection — even offered a fifty percent discount — but rarely succeeded in being paid. No matter what I did, he wanted to try. But when I gave Garlic protection money, he gave nothing. Garlic slapped Curly, and he swallowed his tears, not compromising or telling Iron Ox. At that moment, I was shocked and couldn't understand what was going on in his mind. Until his father came to pick him up, and I saw it all. Curly told his father; his father told Iron Ox; Iron Ox slapped Garlic. The next day, Garlic found an opportunity to slap Curly again. Curly told his father again; his father told Iron Ox again; Iron Ox slapped Garlic's face with his forehand and backhand. The situation repeated three or four times. Iron Ox's punishment for Garlic kept escalating. Garlic couldn't stand it. He had to give up on his revenge. He didn't expect that Curly's father would appear almost every day. No parent did that. My father came to meet Iron Ox once and my mother had no idea where the sports school even was. In Curly's family though, all the family members visited the sports school. They sometimes came together, sometimes individually.

After two months, even Iron Ox couldn't take it any more. He told Curly directly, "Don't ask any of your relatives to come here. This is not a circus troupe." He spoke to Curly's father in a sarcastic tone and with pause, "Your family seems... Pretty... Busy."

Of course, Sissi was the busiest person in the family. When she found out what her son had for lunch, she was not satisfied with the canteen of the sports school, and she complained to her husband for an hour. Her husband remarked if Egghead could eat this or that, why couldn't their son eat it?

"Egghead's mother sells meat. He can eat meat every day!" That's what Sissi thought.

On one occasion, she rode a bicycle to give her son an extra dish. She waited at the exit of the teaching building. Twenty minutes later, the bell rang. She saw the kids rush out of the building like a flood, and she almost drowned. She felt that the kids in front of her were abnormal. They were more like bandits and hooligans. Dark clouds gathered slowly on her face and cleared up the moment when she saw her son.

"Baby!" Sissi waved her arm. "Mom is here!"

"Mom!" Curly squeezed out of the crowd.

"Do you have a death wish?" someone suddenly grabbed Curly's clothes. "Son of bitch!"

"Who are you calling a bitch?" Sissi called toward to the someone.

"Who are you?" someone faced Sissi, nostrils flaring.

"Release your hand," Sissi slapped the someone's arm. "I am his mom; he is my son."

"Your son bumped into me!"

"He didn't mean to."

"I was bumped by your son and he's not going to pay for it?"

"A little collision won't kill you," Curly said.

"Well, let me crash into you once," someone said.

"You dare!" Sissi glowered at the person and stuck out her chest. "I'll take the hit."

I was beside them and kept apologizing to the someone. No one paid me any attention. Because it was lunchtime, food was heaven. Fortunately, one teacher settled the dispute.

"Please! Listen to the teacher. Everyone is hungry. Go for lunch first. If you want to quarrel, do it after lunch," the teacher said.

"What kind of teacher are you?" Sissi rolled her eyes.

"Good-heartedness does not compensate!" the teacher said. "Whether you like to quarrel or not… That's none of my business."

The teacher left.

Sissi went to the canteen with us, sat with us, watched us eat, and asked us to eat all the meat that she brought. She promised that she would bring a dish every day. I became a beneficiary. Chicken, duck, fish, pork, beef, mutton, frog and turtle's cousin: every day was a different dish. I also had the chance to eat donkey and horse meat, and the food didn't taste bad.

My mother began to know more about my life in the sports school from Sissi's complaints. Although Sissi's complaints were not directed at my mother, there were always one or two sentences that made my mother uncomfortable. Such as, "Last night, our family had an argument about sports school. If your son didn't go to the sports school, I wouldn't have let my son go to the sports school, even if someone killed me." My mother felt embarrassed, as if it were all her fault. She argued if Curly could become a sports star, it would all be worth it, and God would bless Curly.

My mother was a Christian, the kind of Christian who went to church every Sunday. Curly's grandma was also a Christian and the one who convinced my mother to believe in God. But she failed to convince her daughter-in-law.

"Here is God. There is Buddha," Sissi said. "Who do I believe in? I don't believe in anybody."

"Don't talk nonsense," my mother said. "Believe in God for eternal life."

"For eternal life? You and my mother-in-law are too optimistic," Sissi said. "I don't want eternal life. I only want my son to be happy and healthy."

"God will bless your son."

"Thank you."

My mother didn't like being too close to people, especially those who did not believe in God. She told me not to eat the food that Curly's mother brought. I asked my mother what I should do when she offered.

"Say you don't want to eat," my mother spoke with ease. She didn't want to owe Sissi any favours. But It was a difficult thing for me. I was the one who had to face the "favours." If I could tell Sissi straight up that my mother told me not to eat the food she brought, things would have been easy.

I couldn't betray my mother. I started to pretend I had a stomach ache. Sissi wanted to take me to see a doctor. Then diarrhoea. What excuse could I make? I could say that I was a vegetarian. What a perfect excuse! But even monks were allowed to eat meat in those days.

Sissi thought my behaviour was a little strange. I only ate

one or two pieces of meat. She wasn't very happy, but she was happy to see her son finish the rest of the meat. Luckily, she had only the body of an adult, not the brain of an adult.

Maybe my mother's prayers were answered. Sissi stopped delivering food because Iron Ox said that Curly was the popular star in the team. Curly didn't quite understand what Iron Ox meant. In front of the whole team, Iron Ox told Curly, "Save your mother's energy and tell her not to come." Teammates followed the coach's lead and heckled him. Curly felt a trace of shame and I nodded gravely. Later, he awkwardly copied and pasted the words exactly to Sissi. The incident triggered his parents' quarrel. What an innocent husband!

Curly was Sissi's whole world. She would tolerate everything and do anything for him. What an incredible mother! When she peeled an apple with a knife, she cut in one continuous line. The peel looked like it was still covered with apple. Usually, the family's toilet paper was the size of a magazine cover. She tore the paper sheets in two. That way, if her son wanted to wipe his ass and his shit was too wet, he could avoid the experience of wiping, folding, and wiping again, a risky thing when the shit can be wiped back on the ass.

My mother asked me not to eat Sissi's food, but she didn't ask me not to take Frank's car. Maybe it was because Frank didn't complain to her about anything. So, I strategically hitchhiked with Frank on school days. Nothing special ever happened — the same place at the same time — until one day, it wasn't the same vehicle.

It was a day before winter vacation, brisk and wet in the coastal city. I wore clothes like a bear. My toes were a little cold because my feet sweat easily. I saw Sissi riding a twenty-six-inch lady's bicycle. Curly was sitting in the back seat and waving to me. I just wanted to start thinking about something else. Sissi called out to me, "Egghead, get on!"

I replayed her words, quickly brainstorming, "Get on what?"

Sissi parked the bicycle beside me. The way Curly was sitting in the back was like sitting on a horse.

"Baby, move forward as far as possible," Sissi said.

Curly wiggled his hips forward under the bicycle cushion. I was a little worried about his penis considering how he was stuck there. If the bicycle cushion suddenly came down… I looked behind Curly at the space he had squeezed out for me. I knew roughly what I was going to do but still waited for Sissi's instructions. For Christ's sake, she only kept me waiting for half a second.

"Egghead! Faster, get on! Hold my son's waist." I obeyed Sissi's orders and pushed Curly a little further into the abyss of the bicycle cushion to get more space to sit. Curly screamed loudly, but not a sound from the pain.

"Hold tight!" Sissi said.

The handlebars wobbled twice and the wheels began to roll. In the morning rush hour, fifty percent of the world's bicycles were here. Sissi was riding very hard, her body swaying back and forth. She kept ringing the bicycle bell, wanting to keep the route smooth. Curly shouted, "Boiling water coming! Get out of the way! We're not responsible for burns!"

The ride went smoothly. We only stopped at a few red lights.

A woman cyclist with a northern appearance was astonished by the picture in front of her. She was twice the width of Sissi. There was a fat boy in her back seat. Her eyes looked admiringly at Sissi. Curly and I stared at the fat boy, trying to frighten him.

"The two boys' weight must be at least one hundred and ten kilograms," the northern accent spat out.

Sissi was panting like a steam train, with smoke coming off her. She had no superfluous breath to speak to anyone. Her lips moved slightly in a smile.

At another red light, a man with a southern accent started speaking to himself, "Oh, twins! Oh, no, it doesn't look like twins."

Curly and I stared at this man, too, trying to frighten him. Finally, we arrived at school five minutes earlier than usual.

At that time, I thought Sissi should switch jobs with my mother. Sissi could sell pork, while my mother could sell vegetables, because she always complained she lacked the strength to chop pork. I thought she was weak because she didn't ride a bike. Yes, my mother was in the empire of bicycles and didn't ride one. She was like a fish in water without being able to swim.

For the next three days, Curly and I squeezed into the crowded bus — it was like packed sardines … for thirty minutes before walking fifteen minutes more to school. Sissi was exhausted. She could squeeze lemon juice out of her thighs. And Frank was in hospital. Somebody had rear-ended him while he was not wearing a seat belt. One of his ribs fractured. I didn't know how serious his condition was.

My mother prayed for Frank and told me that it was thanks to God he recovered.

My father kept his promise to teach me how to ride a bicycle that summer.

Curly didn't know when I learned to ride a bicycle. When he saw me pass him on a twenty-six-inch man's bicycle, he went wild with surprise. The bicycle was adult size, too old and heavy. I had to shake my butt to get on the seat right and stand on my tiptoes to pedal. I knew he would chase my bicycle. I pedalled with all my horsepower. What I didn't know was that he would side jump onto the back seat. I fell to the ground like a confused cowboy. My palm was a little scratched. Curly was totally fine, though. I believe he had the ability to dodge bullets.

I stood up, pointed to Curly and pointed to the bicycle. He gave me a big smile and helped pick up the bicycle quickly. I slapped the top of his head. He was still happy to ask me if he could ride my bicycle. I made a gesture of agreement. He put his right foot on the left pedal of the bicycle.

"Wait," I said. "You can't ride a bicycle, can you?"

"If you can ride, I can ride," Curly said.

"Cut it out!" "I said. He turned and straddled the back seat of my bicycle.

"I don't have the capacity to carry anyone," I said. "My legs can't land at the same time."

"Don't worry," Curly said. "I can hold it steady."

It was as though his buttocks were covered with super glue, impossible to separate from my bicycle. We cooperated very well. The handlebars wobbled badly at first, so he pushed off the road with his legs to help me control the balance, and I gradually became better.

Curly learned to ride a bike later that day. It took him about ten minutes. In the process, the bike fell down twice, the first time resulting in me having to hold the front wheel between my legs and straightening the handlebar.

In the days that followed, we played with the bike as though it were a star and it was almost time for a circus show. The maximum passenger capacity was four people. I wasn't a rider that time, Garlic was. Another sat in the back seat, one on the bicycle frame, and the last one on the handlebars. What an amazing quality. With four people holding on, the bicycle didn't fall apart and successfully completed a circle around the playground.

Most of the time, though, there was only me and Curly. When he straddled the back seat, he was not just a passenger. He stretched out his legs and pushed the pedals. I put my foot on the frame and only controlled the direction. When the bicycle was about to cross the bridge, he would jump out of the seat and change his position, sitting sideways in the back seat. I would put my foot back on the pedal. He put his left hand on my left thigh and his right hand on my right thigh. His hand would push my thigh, and give me extra power. We could take part in tandem bicycle racing or any other competition in double events. Unfortunately, track and field athletes had to fight alone.

Approaching the track meet, Iron Ox shouted slogans — "Friendship first, competition second" ... That's falsehood! In track and field, "the winner takes it all"! In fact, his logic was chaotic. His training techniques were not scientific at all. My long jump talent was much better than my high jump. He forced me to practice high jump, because his was the "high jump" team. Everyone on our team had to start with high jump.

Kitty feared the high jump crossbar. Iron Ox put up the rubber string instead and let her jump. She flew over it like a fairy. Iron Ox changed to the aluminium crossbar and she dared not jump again. Then she went to try long jump. After just one jump, she used the whole night to clean the sand from her shoes. Luckily, her sprint was good.

Fox Eye dared to jump, but she couldn't make any technical moves. Iron Ox described her movement as performed by a dead pig. After various testing, she was deemed only fit for long-distance running.

Garlic was not fit for high jump. Iron Ox changed "high"

into “long” for him.

Curly had the same problem as Fox Eye. He was frustrated that he couldn’t train high jump with me, but was very willing to run with Kitty. He was shocked when he could not beat Kitty in a race. I was pretty envious of his simple and direct training. But at that time, high jump was considered the most promising event in track and field. See, in 1984, there was a Shanghainese who broke the world record for high jump in Eberstadt, Germany. We called him the “High Jump Prince”. That was the power of idols. They represented China, just like table tennis, pandas and the Great Wall.

I had never wondered where my athletic ability came from. Normally, in the municipal athletics meet, more than a dozen other sports schools came to participate. I was always in the top three, usually placing third. But I never won a championship, not once. The closest I came was when, luckily, the champion was injured, and I came in second.

Curly missed his first race because of me. Iron Ox put me in charge of guiding him, but no one told me the time of the race, and I thought Curly would remind me, but he didn’t. Iron Ox was busy, and I knew he wouldn’t punish me. He needed me to be in a good mood to compete.

“Never mind,” he consoled me, as easy-going as a sheep. “Have a good rest and prepare for your event.”

That afternoon, the sky was blue and clouds were white. The day was breezy and warm. What a perfect day for a meet! I felt a little sleepy. I wanted Iron Ox to hit me on the head with his finger as in training, but he totally disappointed me. He became a civilized gentleman. I had to slap myself on the thighs and face. The effect was not good. I needed strength from anger and pain. That’s why I always did better in training than in competition. In the end, I won sixth place for my age group. Iron Ox’s face looked as if it had been ironed.

CHAPTER VII

Our school ushered in a new term, and I lost a classmate — Pony. I was a little depressed. He was a very generous person, not like Doorbell. When Doorbell repeated a grade, I set off two firecrackers to celebrate.

Pony was different from Doorbell. One was the star in the sky. The other was the dust on the ground. One had a father who was a sailor, always onboard, and a mother who loved to dance. The other had a father who was a gangster, always in prison, and a mother who remarried. One liked reading kung fu novels. The other only read comic books.

Last year, Pony's grades were normal. This year, he gave up completely. I gave him assignment answers to copy, and he thanked me politely, but he was too lazy to copy. He always shared some delicious snacks with me and brought new gadgets to satisfy my desire for novelty. It was frustrating not to be in the same classroom with him any more. Fortunately, we were not far from each other, only thirty seconds away. The distance between Pony and Doorbell was only a ninety-degree turn.

Doorbell usually ate at his grandparents' house. After dinner, he went back to his house where no one was. Within thirty square metres, there was a single bed, a double sofa, a fourteen-inch black-and-white TV set on the dining table, some basic kitchen and toilet appliances, and the rest was just a mess. This was a very spacious space for a child.

Pony hated strangers smoking in his house, especially when

his father went to sea. Soon, he moved in with Doorbell. In order to improve his quality of life, he moved his father's VCR to Doorbell's apartment. But Doorbell's TV made him feel like he was colour-blind. He took advantage when the ashtray was fullest at home, and his father went to sea. In front of his mother, he and Doorbell took the twenty-nine-inch colour TV away. Gradually, he moved what he needed to Doorbell's apartment. He also turned from a guest into a host. Except for the bedframe, he threw everything on the floor and asked his father to mail a new mattress, quilt and pillow all made in USA.

Doorbell was glad to have Pony. His quality of life improved greatly. His horizons began to broaden. He saw several foreign movies and many Hong Kong swordsman series. He felt like he saw more of the world than the Hubble space telescope. Pony had several new movies almost every week. There was one movie which they watched together.

On the TV screen, a helicopter flew over the blue sea. A white man with a six pack was surfing and flipping in the waves.

"So cool!" Doorbell said.

"This is America," Pony said.

With the camera angle switching, the helicopter had a bird's eye view of the beach. A group of blondes in bikinis played volleyball on a golden beach.

"So open!" Doorbell said.

"This is America," Pony said.

The angle switched again, and the blondes were topless, recorded in slow motion heading for the sea. They rushed, in slow motion, into the arms of men returning from surfing.

"So..." Doorbell was speechless.

"This is America," Pony said.

Doorbell's spirit of generosity grew. Whether it was difficult or not to share, he didn't forget his boys who peeped in the women's toilet. He realized that the mystery they had known from the women's toilet was nothing compared to the American videotape.

Following the peeping incident, a topic circulated among Doorbell and his group — a buttock with a birthmark. Someone said the birthmark look like a heart; someone said it look like a cloud; someone drew a pattern on a piece of paper, and someone revised it. No one knew who had seen it. All the peepers said they saw it. People who weren't involved in the peeping also started talking about that birthmark.

Almost all female athletes were concerned about their butt's reputation, but they were very generous, not shy. They went through many competitions, and their psychological quality was very strong. When a sportswoman was in a good mood, she would ask, "Would you like to see my ass?"

The sportsman's answer would always be, "YES!"

She would say, "Dream on!" When she was in a bad mood, she would say, "Go back to see your mother's ass, asshole!"

When the peeping incident was exposed in our team, it became a forbidden topic. Iron Ox investigated us. He struck each of the guys' head on the team, but the power dynamic was different this time. To me it felt like a raindrop, unaffected. Curly pretended to complain of pain. Garlic got a knock and spat out, "Sonuvabitch." Iron Ox raised his hand and stared at Garlic. Garlic raised his head and stared back. Iron Ox changed his gesture, pointed at Garlic and warned him to try that again. Garlic angrily told Iron Ox to try that again! Iron Ox satisfied Garlic's wish. But Garlic neither waited to be hit, nor escaped. He raised his arm quickly, forcefully and successfully blocked Iron Ox's attack. It was obvious that he was not a peeper.

Curly asked me why Iron Ox doubted him. I said it was because he looked like a chimpanzee. Actually, I didn't know why. Sometimes, reasons are just random bullshit.

Throughout the whole process, the sportswomen in our team were standing by. Some of them ate melon seeds. Some ate plums. Some ate sliced fruit, while others chewed gum. They all took pleasure in the guys' misfortune. But one of them was abnormal. She stood by quietly, not eating, talking or laughing. She was even a little nervous. She was supposed to be the least nervous woman on earth — Fox Eye. I suspected Fox Eye was the Cinderella everybody was looking for. I told Curly, he ran straight to Fox Eye like Columbus who discovered the New World. "Egghead told me. You're the butt with a birthmark."

Wordlessly, Fox Eye went to the Iron Ox. I saw her pointing at me, and her lips moved three times. Then, Iron Ox roared my name. The sound penetrated the playground. With an innocent face, I went to Iron Ox. He hit me hard. I thought he wanted to open me like a watermelon. And he backhand slapped me, hard. I was spinning almost like a top. There was liquid running out of my eyes and mouth. Tears didn't matter. When my finger touched the corner of my mouth, I saw red. I became like an irrational bull, and bumped my head into Iron Ox's chest. He sank to the ground. Then I screamed and ran.

Iron Ox froze up for a second, and then shouted an order at all our teammates to catch me. I ran a few steps and stopped. I spat blood on the grass-less ground. I turned around and faced whoever was chasing me. Garlic was the first and locked my neck with his arm. I pulled down his arm with all my strength and bit into it deep. He grabbed my hair and threw me to the ground. He put his left and right knees on my arms. I looked like I was nailed to a cross. I was also like a fish jumping ashore, shaking my body desperately, trying to break free. I didn't know who was holding my foot down, at least two other bastards joined. And someone flicked my penis and balls.

"Let him stand up," Iron Ox commanded.

"Who touched my brother!" I spat a little blood.

"Do you know you're wrong?" Iron Ox asked.

"Can you tell me I'm wrong?" I asked. "Who touched my brother!"

"What sort of attitude is that?" Garlic asked and his arm almost locked me again.

"Leave him alone," Iron Ox said.

My eyes fell on Curly, expecting him to give me a hint. Instead, he pretended to look elsewhere. Fox Eye pointed quietly at Curly.

"You moron!" I rushed in front of Curly and slapped him and again with my backhand.

Curly covered his face and kicked me in the stomach. Iron Ox was seizing my arm to hold me back as I jumped up, preparing to give Curly a flying kick.

"Take him to my office!" Iron Ox ordered two guys. "The rest are free to go."

My ears were filled with cheers celebrating the triumph of justice.

Iron Ox left me in the office, gave me paper and pen, and asked me to write a letter of confession. I asked him, write what? He let me wait and he left the office. After a few minutes, Iron Ox, Doorbell and his coach, along with other peepers and their coaches were all in the office.

"Did he join?" Iron Ox pointed at me.

"Join what?" Doorbell blinked his eyes.

"Come here," Doorbell's coach said to him. "Open your

palm."

I saw Doorbell's coach taking a drag of his cigarette, then hold Doorbell's wrist as he burned it in Doorbell's palm until it went out.

"Did he join?" Doorbell's coach pointed at me.

"I don't know!" Doorbell gave me a pained smile.

"Did he join?" Doorbell's coach scanned the others.

The other peepers' coach asked same question. All the answers were, "I don't know."

Iron Ox let other coaches and peepers leave. He closed the door and took out a bottle of Pepsi-Cola from the refrigerator. He lit a cigarette and said, "I'm glad you didn't join them, but you shouldn't slap Curly. You must apologize to him."

I drank the Cola and my mood was much better.

"He grabbed my penis," I said.

"No matter what he does, you can't beat him. You should tell me, and I will punish him," Iron Ox said. "Did you hear what I said?"

With the sound of my burp, I said I knew, and told Iron Ox I wanted another drink. He didn't fulfil my wish. He said drinking too much was not good for my height. He tapped me on my shoulder, indicating it was time to leave. I followed him as he gathered up my teammates who had scattered across the playground. He even told us to number off from left to right. Unfortunately, we couldn't number off like soldiers. We repeated it more than ten times until Iron Ox was satisfied. He ordered Curly and me to stand out and began his speech: "Coaches are usually harder than athletes, because a coach has to guide more than one athlete. In the face of a number of athletes, even coaches can't observe every detail." After his fantastic speech, he looked at me and waved his chin toward Curly. I was not going to hide my wisdom in this solemn moment.

"Please accept my sincerest apologies," I said.

"Who are you apologizing to?" Iron Ox asked.

"Curly!" I said.

"Your attitude is very good. I forgive you," Iron Ox said. Then asked Curly, "How about you?"

"Me what?" Curly asked.

"It seems that someone is not aware of his mistake," Iron Ox nodded. "Who can remind him?"

No one dared to speak.

"Let me remind you," Iron Ox said and give Curly a knock on the head. "You touched his lower body."

Tears welled up in Curly's eyes. I didn't know why. He should feel itchy and laugh, because the knock from Iron Ox seemed like a mosquito.

"This is the most vulnerable and important part of a man," Iron Ox pointed at my private parts. "If it is harmed, no amount of money can compensate!"

I had a very naughty idea at that moment because I was bored. I thought, "What if I took my pants off?" Of course, I was wearing underpants — I wasn't stupid enough to strip myself naked.

"Fortunately, nothing happened today! You two. You and you," Iron Ox continued, interrupting my thought. He pointed at me, Curly, Garlic and Fox Eye. "The four of you — write letters of confession."

"Why me!" The only lady felt it was unfair.

"Why you? You go home and think about it. Without you, without everything… You have to be responsible for what you say," Iron Ox concluded. "To finish off, everyone, ten laps of endurance running! Egg Head, stay."

That was the most wonderful moment. I watched them gasp like Alaskan sled dogs. "Hallelujah!" was ringing in my heart. "Come on, speed up!" That was my sound to refuel them.

When they finished the fifth lap, Iron Ox ordered me to lead the run. I knew he wouldn't let me be too comfortable.

"Too slow, Egg Head!" When we finished the sixth lap, Iron Ox said, "Fox Eye, you take the lead."

"Egg Head, if you fall out of the top three, run five more laps!" When we finished the seventh lap, Iron Ox said, "Who's slower than Egg Head! Three more laps!"

What a wicked arrangement!

"Slow down!" Garlic ran up and whispered at Fox Eye, "Are you deaf?"

If Fox Eye had entered her rhythm, she could have kept that pace until the earth was destroyed. Garlic had no choice but to pull her ponytail. This worked. Fox Eye dared not shout. She protested in a low voice, "Iron Ox, look at me!"

"Too slow!" after the eighth lap, Iron Ox warned, "Curly, if you are lapped by Fox Eye, you will see how I treat you."

Curly didn't care at all. Like a dead pig who was not afraid of boiling water, his pace was like walking on the moon. Eventually, he was lapped by everyone and no one got an extra lap. Only he got a real knock on the head from Iron Ox.

It was probably too hot. The sunset glow baked half the sky red. The air was humid, no wind at all. Even the cicadas in the trees were numb.

Curly returned home by himself. He went into the bedroom and threw himself face down on the bed. Sissi was busy cooking dinner in the kitchen and yelled a few things like, "Have you washed your hands? Are you hungry? We will have dinner when your father comes back! There's half a watermelon in the fridge!"

Sissi turned down the gas and went into the bedroom. She affectionately patted Curly on the hip, "Don't sleep in bed without taking a shower."

"Leave me alone!" Curly said.

"When your dad comes home and sees you like this... Let him give you a lesson," Sissi went back to the kitchen.

Since Frank couldn't commute by car, he had to commute by bike. He couldn't adapt himself very well to such change, and he had to carry his bicycle upstairs and downstairs every day in case of thieves.

"Your son is smelly," Sissi greeted Frank when he opened the door. They were her first words to welcome him.

"What's going on?" Frank went into the bedroom. He saw Curly sleeping on the bed like a climber, and he asked some questions about the training. Curly didn't say a word. Frank gently tugged at Curly's ear and asked, "Didn't you bring your ears home?"

"Leave me alone!" Curly shouted.

"Come out for dinner." Sissi's voice was flying in the bedroom.

"Get up," Frank patted Curly's on the butt. "After dinner, take a shower and go to bed."

"Are you deaf?" Curly ranted. "I said, leave me alone!"

"I am deaf?" Frank spanked Curly hard. "How dare you speak to me like that?"

Curly jumped out of bed. He gritted his teeth and glared at Frank. Sissi walked in and took Curly's hand as if nothing had happened. Curly shook off her hand and shouted, "Get the hell out of here!"

"How dare you speak to your mother like that!" Frank spanked Curly two more times.

"You both only know how to hit me!" Curly cried.

"Don't hit my son," Sissi interrupted. "Calm down. No need to be so angry."

After Frank pulled out a cigarette and it turned to ash, Curly spat out everything, including two slaps in his face from me as it should be.

CHAPTER VIII

The next day, when I met Curly, I felt sorry and tried ass-kissing as best I could. If there was a flattery competition on earth, I wouldn't let anyone else win the championship.

That evening, I finished my training and went home. The temperature outside was thirty-five degrees, but I felt like I was walking into a cellar. My mother's face looked like someone owed her millions, my father was drinking his fifty-two percent alcohol. Normally, when my mother saw me coming home, she would tell me to drink flush juice, or give me a slice of watermelon. Then, she'd prepare dishes for me. But that day, she treated me as if I weren't born from her. I was told some bullshit when I was very young. I had asked her where I came from, and she said I was picked up from a trash can. For this reason, I was really sad for a long time and was well behaved.

"I am thirsty!" I said.

"Drink tap water," my father said.

I opened the refrigerator and found nothing. When I turned on the tap water, my mother stopped me and poured me a glass of cold boiled water from the kettle. I drank it all in one breath.

"I am hungry!" I said.

"There is rice in the pot. Serve yourself," my mother said.

I shrugged and filled a big bowl of rice. I sat down with my bowl in my hand, and just as I started to move my chopsticks, I ate my father's backhand slap. I covered my face and looked at my father. He looked at me in contempt. I turned to my mother.

She pretended she didn't see anything. I put the bowl on the table and made some noise. My father's hand went up again. I quickly backed away from his attack and shouted, "What did I do?"

"Did you slap Curly?" my mother asked.

"He kicked me first!" I skipped over the part about Curly touching my penis. It was difficult to say.

"You are such a thoughtless child!" my mother said. "His parents are so kind to you. How dare you slap his face!"

"He kicked me first!" I still skipped over the key reason.

"Sissi cried when she told me," my mother said. "You made us lose face!"

"Come here," my father wavcd to me very gently.

I knew it was a trap, but I had to move. My father could easily catch me at this distance. I didn't want him to waste too much energy, it wouldn't do me any good. I put two hands on my face and looked at him through my fingers.

"Put your hands down," my father's tone was calm. I hesitated for a moment. If he wanted to hit me, my whole body, except my face, was defenceless. I slowly put down my hands. A forehand slap hit me like lightning.

"Fuck you!" I blurted.

"That's enough," my mother stood up, separating me from my father. "Let him eat first."

During that meal, I didn't need soup, because I had enough tears to drink. My mother thought that I deserved to be beaten, but she didn't ask me to apologize to Curly. She told me to keep my distance from him.

I followed my mother's wish. When I saw Curly on the playground, I pretended not see him. Curly didn't know what was happening and he thought I was the same person as yesterday who kissed his ass. He even slapped me on the scalp as a greeting.

"Stay away from me!" I said. "You piece of trash."

Curly didn't notice any change in my attitude. He began to recite the poem about me. The people who created this poem were geniuses. "Egg Head, Egg Head, no worries about the rain, People have umbrellas, I have Egg Head." Curly pulled out a handful of melon seeds from his trousers pocket and tried to share with me. I didn't even move a finger. He wanted to put a melon seed in my mouth. I spit in his face. He wiped his face with his clothes, and suddenly hit me in the deltoid. The best muscle in the arm is the deltoid. When it's attacked, you feel pain, but not too much pain. I also punched him in the deltoid. He threw a punch. Then I threw a punch. Back and forth. Our fists became heavier and heavier. After thirteen rounds, our angel of peace showed up.

"What are you doing?" Kitty asked. She saw Curly clenching his teeth with tears in his eyes. "Stop it, Egg Head! Otherwise, I'll tell Iron Ox."

"Fuck off! You brainless cow!" My voice was very monotonous.

"What's happening?" Kitty asked Curly.

"I don't know," Curly said. "He is a psycho!"

"Yes, he is indeed!" Kitty said.

"You dumbass! Are you in love with him?" I pointed at Kitty and pointed at Curly. "Last time he hit you in the breast. Do you want to thank him for helping your development?"

"You are right!" Kitty said and faced Curly. "You must have provoked Egg Head first."

"I gave him melon seeds and he spat in my face," Curly said.

"Who punched first?" Kitty asked.

"Him!" I said and told Kitty what happened last night.

"You are not a man!" Kitty sighed at Curly.

"He has no hair on his balls!" I said.

"Neither do you!" Curly said.

"You're wrong! I have hair!" I said.

"Prove it to me!" Curly said.

"You two are nuts," Kitty said. "If I stay around you, I'm going to be dumb."

"You are a cow without brains," I said.

"I agree!" Curly said.

Kitty snorted in disgust and left.

I told Curly there were unwritten rules in sports schools. Men fight, even if it's an unfair fight. We should not tell the coaches. It was absolutely forbidden to tell parents. Only girls were bullied by boys and could tell their coaches. Almost no girls told their parents. I gave him an example from when I fought with someone else. My nose was beaten till it bled. The coach saw it. It was clear that it wasn't bleeding from too much chocolate, but I would say I hit a streetlamp, or my feet slipped.

That night, Curly copied and pasted my words to Sissi. He wanted to teach her a lesson. But he was too specific when he told her what had happened that afternoon. Sissi didn't get the point. She only knew that I had bullied her son again.

"I am going to see your coach tomorrow," she said.

"You are not allowed to go," Frank said.

"You just like to make trouble," Curly said.

Sissi put the dishes on the table and cried, "You two have no conscience at all! I wash your clothes, cook meals, fold quilts and clean the house. What do I get? Thankless attitudes!"

The following day, Sissi told Curly to rest at home for a day and play some video games, watch cartoons, eat watermelon and ice cream. She went on her own to the playground. What stuck in her mind was that I slapped her son in the face.

She went to the place where the coaches gathered and told Iron Ox what had happened. Iron Ox didn't say anything. He walked out of the office and found me. His voice came to my ears at the speed of light, then he raised his hand to me. I was like a happy dog that saw bones and flew towards him. When I saw Sissi, my sixth sense answered why I wasn't seeing Curly. No sooner had she seen me than she began to cry. Her voice trembled and asked why I slapped her son in the face. What if something happened to her son to make him deaf or retarded? She admitted that her son was sometimes unlovable. However, for thirteen years, she and her husband spanked their son but never slapped him in the face. She emphasized that no one ever slapped her son in the face. If any unexpected misfortune happened to her son, she would no longer live.

Iron Ox thought that with my wisdom, I could handle this situation. He didn't realize that I was dumb as a woodcock. He had to do me a favour. He pushed me in front of Sissi and asked her to slap me in the face.

Sissi's tears sparkled in her eyes. She shook her head and said that she didn't want to slap me. She wanted me to slap her, not her son.

Iron Ox asked me questions to which he should have known the answers. "How many times did you slap Curly?"

"Twice." It was a real problem for me, so Sissi answered for me.

"You, Curly or me, who will slap him twice in return?" Iron Ox asked Sissi.

"No need for that," Sissi said.

"That's letting Egg Head off too easy!" Doorbell's coach joined in the fun. "At least let him slap himself and see how much sincerity he has."

"This is not a bad idea," Iron Ox agreed. He lifted his chin and ordered, "Do it!"

I hesitated for half a second, closed my left eye and slapped my left face with my left hand.

"Too gentle!" Doorbell's coach said.

I tried hard.

"Still!" Doorbell's coach said.

"Fuck you!" I roared and began slapping myself nonstop. At that moment, I thought my father's slap was not as tough as mine.

Iron Ox stopped me when I slapped myself the fifth time.

"Are you all satisfied?" I shouted with a snotty nose, runny eyes and a slight cough.

Youth means that after sleeping, everything recovers and is forgotten. But this time, it wasn't. I began to listen to my mother's advice and kept Curly at arm's length.

Shortly after, Fox Eye started an underground romance with Doorbell. They did a good job of keeping the secret. Only tiny birds in the sky and wildflowers on the ground knew they were in love.

Since Fox Eye took a very roundabout way to find out her ass had been seen by Doorbell, she had an intense mental struggle. She wanted to find someone to pour her heart out. But there seemed to be nothing to say. She didn't feel pain or loss. The only real feeling was that she was very curious about the details of the whole thing. She wrote a line on a small piece of paper, crumpled it small like a snot-ball and found a chance to throw it at Doorbell during class.

Doorbell saw something fly past him, land on the table, bounce twice and roll to the ground. He turned along the parabola and saw that Fox Eye winked at him and looked at the floor. He stepped on the paper ball quickly and pretended to tie his shoelaces. He tore it carelessly when he opened the paper ball. He put the two pieces of paper together as if they were a treasure map.

Keep it secret and wait for me at the grocery after training tonight. Doorbell received the information on paper, turned to Fox Eye, put the paper in his mouth and swallowed it. Fox Eye glanced at him and pretended not to know him. Doorbell stuck out his tongue and proved nothing.

That night, Doorbell waited for Fox Eye for two hours. He drank three bottles of orange soda and one bottle of beer. His coach always ended training at the earliest time. Fox Eye's coach did the opposite and she waited until everyone was gone. She rode her bicycle past him and said, "Follow me!"

Doorbell jumped on his bicycle and chased her to a dark, secluded alley. They stood face to face but could not see each other clearly. His breathing was a little short. The alcohol made him feel a little dizzy. Hormones rolled in his body. A breeze blew through, carrying the body odour from Fox Eye.

"Why did you do that?" her voice was as cold as ice but could not cool down Doorbell. He felt horny, suddenly embraced her, and the lower part of his body became as hard as a stick, like a hotdog between two bodies.

"Dirty bastard!"

Fox Eye didn't raise her right knee seriously, but enough to make Doorbell moan in pain and hear him say, "I like you!"

She froze for a moment and thought Doorbell would say "sonuvabitch" or pull her hair. She could accept that, but why this? She suddenly found a picture in her mind from TV — a girl slapped a boy in the face. The boy still said that he liked the girl, but that was it.

"What do you like about me?" She didn't want to have her

first confession of attraction to end up like that.

"I like everything about you." When Doorbell was horny, he could say anything you wanted to hear and do anything you wanted done.

"Like my ass?"

"No, I just saw the birthmark, but I didn't know it was you."

"So, you didn't like my ass?"

"No. I mean yes... But no... You know."

"I know what?" Fox Eye said. "You are an asshole?"

"Yes, I am an asshole!" Doorbell said. "I should have died in that iron ball accident."

That was a good shot. She began to pity him, and her psychological defences began to retreat. When she got home that night, while her father was taking a bath, she asked her mother why she married her father. Her mother said, "Marry a chicken; follow a chicken. Marry a dog; follow a dog. I have made my bed. Now I lie in it."

Fox Eye's attitude towards Doorbell was like that of master and slave. Everyone knew that a tiger's butt can't be touched. Similarly, Fox Eye's butt couldn't be watched. That was the revenge of the tigress. The truth, though, was that they had already kissed in private.

Every girl has beautiful expectations for the first date. Fox Eye wanted Doorbell's hand glued to her hand tenderly, but his hands moved up and down like thieves. She wanted him to kiss her gently, but he put his tongue into her mouth like a snake. She wanted him to hold her waist gently face to face, but he liked to hold her breasts from behind. She wanted to watch some tender and romantic movies, he invited her to his home and made her wish come true, but as she snuggled up to him contentedly, he started playing another movie. On the screen, there was a helicopter flying over a blue sea. A foreign man with a six pack was surfing and flipping in the waves…

Fox Eye's mother found her daughter's period was not on time. Her head consumed with an uneasy sense of foreboding. This bad feeling became stronger with each passing day. Three days later, she told her husband, and her husband said it was normal to be two or three days late. Five days later, she bought pregnancy test. The test result from her daughter was positive. She told her husband. Her husband asked for another test. She told him their daughter did another test, and he asked if she had tested it herself. She nodded and shook her head with tears, "Why our daughter?" Her husband grabbed her daughter's hair roughly and shook three times.

When I first saw Fox Eye's father, I was so frightened. But that time, my breathing stopped for another reason. I had never seen Iron Ox look like that. He asked me to bring Kitty and Curly to the office. The moment I turned around; I breathed a sigh of relief. It didn't seem to be my problem. When the three of us arrived at the office, Iron Ox asked Curly and me to wait outside. Curly asked me what had happened. I didn't really want to talk to him. I told him that he asked me the same question I was going to ask. Through the window, I saw Iron Ox's eyebrows twist into knots. It seemed that this matter made him very anxious. I asked Curly what had happened. The bastard gave me the answer that I gave him.

"If nothing happened, what are you doing here?" I asked.

"If nothing happened, what are you doing here?" Curly asked.

"What a lazy bastard!" I said.

"What a lazy bastard!" Curly said.

"Oh, shit!"

I decided to stop speaking, but I still got his, "Oh, shit."

Kitty came out and Curly was called in. I asked Kitty what had happened. Kitty said she didn't know. Her eyes told me that she really didn't know.

"What did you say in the office?" I asked.

"They asked me if I knew anything about Fox Eye," Kitty said. "The man is her father."

"Curly bullying Fox Eye?" I thought aloud, and answered myself in a whisper, "that's impossible." I asked, "How many days has she been absent?"

"About three days," Kitty said.

"It's your turn." Curly came out with a very relaxed look.

"What did you say to them?" I asked.

"I said you bullied Fox Eye," Curly said.

"This is no joke!" I said.

"What are you doing?" Iron Ox's voice pierced my body and I began to move.

"Don't worry! I didn't say anything about you," Curly admitted.

"You two can leave," Iron Ox said. "You, come in and close the door."

I sat on the chair as ordered. Fox Eye's father offered me a cigarette. Meanwhile, Iron Ox gave me a bottle of coke. I took the cigarette and coke. I wanted to say I didn't smoke and I wanted to know when I could drink, but I didn't know what I should do. Iron Ox solved my problem, he took the cigarette out of my hand and began to smoke. I slowly put my mouth close to the coke.

"What do you know about Fox Eye's relationship with Doorbell?" Iron Ox asked.

"I don't understand," I looked blankly at him.

"Don't answer so quickly. Think about it," Iron Ox said.

"What kind of relationship?" I asked.

"Did they get very close?" Iron Ox asked.

"I didn't see that."

"Did you hear anything?" Iron Ox asked.

"I didn't hear anything."

"Don't rush to answer."

Iron Ox faced Fox Eye's father, "Do you have any questions for him?"

"Did you see them together?" Fox Eye's father asked.

"I'm not in the same class as them," I told him.

"It's true. The previous two were in the same class as your daughter," Iron Ox explained.

"So, no one knew they were together," Fox Eye's father said. "My daughter lied to me!"

"She may have been threatened," I blurted out. It suddenly occurred to me that Fox Eye cared a lot about her ass.

"What do you mean?" Iron Ox asked.

"I mean, you know, the toilet," I stammered.

"What toilet?" Fox Eye's father asked.

"I see. Take your coke," Iron Ox said. "You can go now."

I took the coke and went back to the playground. Curly ran to me eagerly. I didn't share a drop with him. As usual, when Doorbell and I passed one another, we didn't look very friendly at each other. But I didn't realize that was the last time I would see him.

After that, I heard different pieces of his story. He was handcuffed when he was taken away by the police. That evening, around a dozen guys were watching porn at his home. They were also taken to the police station. He was brought to court and charged with rape. The defence lawyer hired by government said

Doorbell had reached the age of fourteen, and requested the judge to convict and impose heavier punishment. The judge took the lawyer's advice, found Doorbell guilty and gave him seven years imprisonment.

Fox Eye transferred to another school during that period.

CHAPTER IX

Autumn and Winter, Spring and Summer — I didn't want to admit that I was growing up so fast. Only two centimetres away from my body's full height prediction (—one hundred and seventy-eight centimetres)— I was soon going to reach my limit. My coach thought that I didn't have a future in high jump, because my height was not high enough to jump higher, and my bouncing power was not like a flea. I agreed with my coach. Most of my opponents were a head taller than me, although they only had longer necks. The good news was that my long jump ability was still very strong. My coach finally saw it, and he had me practice the long jump, throw the javelin, jump over hurdles, and run the one thousand five hundred metres from time to time. He was the most intelligent coach in the world. He was going to make me a pentathlete, because in another six months, when I entered senior high school, my age would allow me to participate in that competition. Actually, I was quite good at the discipline. Around the same time, Curly was chosen to enter a more professional sports school to receive professional sprint training. Both of us would be leaving this semi-professional sports school. Before Curly and I parted ways, our brotherhood had long been reconciled. Our farewell lunch was Kentucky Fried Chicken. That was our favourite.

The senior high school where I enrolled had a college enrolment rate that was top three in Shanghai. Celebrities who graduated from the school included the most powerful person's nephew and several football players. My coach was responsible for my future. He wanted me to get a better education, he said my chances of becoming a professional athlete were almost nil.

These kinds of key senior high schools had educators fully implement and obey the party's quality-oriented education policy to cultivate the creativity of students and educate the socialist builders and successors with a well-rounded development of morality, intelligence, physics and arts. So, I was the one who would entertain their boring learning atmosphere. But we had a deal. I wasn't their real student. My student status was still at the sports school. After the senior high school courses, if I were admitted to a university, I would receive the diploma of this school. If I were unsuccessful, though, I would receive the diploma of sports school. What a fair deal.

Such first-class educational institutions had a very strict test score requirements. Ninety-six percent of the students entered the school by virtue of their own performance. Although I had a special talent, my father still gave Iron Ox some commission which cost him three months' salary. It stressed me out the whole time. But when I heard that someone had donated money to construct a new teaching building, which allowed his children to enter the school, I felt relaxed all of a sudden.

It was generally known that I was the best student in the sports school. After entering the high school, however, I scored the lowest on the proficiency test. There were twelve classes in my grade, a total of six hundred and twenty-four students. It was because of me that my class had the lowest average of the whole grade. My head teacher went crazy. She had just graduated from a first-class university and passed the teacher's professional examination to become a teacher. I became her nightmare, and it was only the beginning.

On the third day of school, in PE class, I fought with a guy in Senior Three for a basketball court. That guy was ten centimetres taller than me. He was not an athlete. He was the kind of child who studied well, was spoiled and liked feeling cool. He thought that because he was the oldest student with a cool bald head, everyone should be afraid of him. That was usually the case, and so he had some attendants. With me, no one knew me, and so no one would cheer for me. He pushed me first and I stepped back one pace. Then I punched him. When he saw his nose bleeding, he was as nervous as a sea cucumber and asked me how I could beat people. There were dozens of people watching. His attendants asked me the same moronic questions. His PE teacher sent us to the disciplinary office. There was such a place in this school. Both our head teachers were present. The discipline teacher didn't know what had happened and there wasn't a surveillance video. He could only judge by his instinct and what we said. What was good for me was that my opponent was older, taller and stronger than me. It was his bald head that especially made him look rebellious and he was emotionally charged. I acted very innocent. In the end, we were both given verbal warnings. This caused my head teacher to lose sleep again. She called my family, and she was so touched by my mother's sincerity that she almost went to church. She told me that my mother had given her some life questions to think about. She also understood what kind of family environment I grew up in. That wasn't bad, but she thought that I still had to study hard and to go to university in the future.

I shouldn't have asked her what my mother said to her, because it would be easier to ask my mother by myself. But I couldn't help it.

"Your mother only wishes you to be healthy and honest. As

for whether you will be successful in the future, follow God's will," my head teacher said.

What a wish: "health and honesty", but no mention of happiness, probably because I was already too happy. In any case, my mother did a good job by accident. Then, my head teacher thought my mother was very westernized. She asked about my mother's job.

At that time, the era of market economy, you were considered rich as long as you had money to buy as much pork as you liked. Private businesses were everywhere. My mother's job had no advantage, so she had been laid off. The government gave her very small welfare payment to survive. Millions of people had been laid off. Sissi was one of them, too.

"Laid off worker," I said.

My head teacher didn't ask for details. She arranged for a boy who studied very well to be my desk mate. By coincidence, he was the tallest boy in class. I ranked third or fifth in height. I didn't care; I was already one hundred and eighty-two centimetres. My height prediction had been bullshit. So, I had to sit in the last row, otherwise I would block the view for other students. My desk mate was not satisfied with the last row. His name was Frank, too. There were so many Franks on the earth, sometimes even their mothers couldn't tell who was whom.

I called him Frank Jr. He was as thin as a bamboo stick and he stooped slightly. He wore lenses as thick as the bottom of a beer bottle. He complained a lot about sitting in the last row because he often couldn't see clearly what the teacher had written on the blackboard. I quite liked my seat because it was convenient for me to take a nap. Frank Jr. always woke me up, and told me this was class time, not sleeping time. After that, he would ask me what the teacher had written on the blackboard.

My eyesight was similar to that of an eagle, but unfortunately, I couldn't always understand what the teacher was writing. Especially our English teacher. His writing was terrible. All the letters were linked together. I could only see the general picture; the rest was up to Frank Jr. to guess for himself. I really hated him interrupting my nap. I had to leave home at seven a.m. for school, go directly to sports school at four p.m., arrive home around seven p.m. and then eat, bath and study! This nerd Frank Jr. just couldn't figure out how tired I was.

The learning gap between me and my classmates, it was just like the sports gap between them and me. They didn't need to take sports seriously. There was no subject such as sports on the college entrance examination. But I had to take cultural courses seriously.

My head teacher happened to coincide with me on this point. She really cared about me. She went to talk to the PE teacher about my stopping PE lessons to give me more time to study. She figured that there were three PE lessons a week. If these hours were spent on studying, the gains would accumulate over time. But the PE teacher disagreed. His dignity would not allow it to happen. My head teacher emphasized that I was a sports student and I had to train all the time. So, it didn't matter if I attended PE lessons. My head teacher was telling the truth, but it triggered my PE teacher's sensitive nerves. He said that no student in the history of the school had ever been treated like this, and if according to her logic, sports students would not have to take PE lessons, then cultural students would not have to take cultural lessons. The PE teacher did a marvellous job. My head teacher was petrified. The PE teacher had a self-satisfied smirk on his face. That kind of person is easily turned on by such a small achievement.

"A sports student? I haven't seen any sports students who was qualified to not take PE classes. Can he or she gets full marks in every PE skill?" PE teacher sneered.

My head teacher was totally defeated. She was too frustrated to tell me what had happened. I was very grateful to her for her efforts. I asked her if she could tell me the criteria for a full score in the PE course. She smiled at me and said, "Forget it." I insisted on knowing the qualifications. She was moved by me and thought that I wanted to set goals. Actually, I was just curious.

When I saw the scoring criteria for PE, I asked, "Is that it?"

"Can I wear spiked shoes?" I asked.

"What do you mean?" There was a doubtful smile on my head teacher's face.

"If I can't wear spiked shoes," I started, "I'll be a little tired when I get full marks for every PE skill."

"What do you mean?"

"I mean that I will get full marks for every skill."

"Are you sure?"

"I am sure."

"Okay, I trust you." She didn't look like she did.

"I need to wear spiked shoes."

"Okay, let me arrange it," she said. "What else do you want?"

"Nothing."

"Okay," she said. "You are sure?"

"With one thousand percent certainty!"

"Okay, let me arrange it," she checked. "Nothing else is needed?"

"No!"

Two days later, in PE class, the wind was gentle and the sun radiant. The weather was glorious. The playground was full of the students who had PE class. There were classes in Grade One, Grade Two and Grade Three. Boys in my class played basketball and football; girls played volleyball and chatted in the shade. I did a twenty-minute warm-up exercise and put on my sports equipment. With spiked shoes on my feet, Adidas's track shorts and a tank top, I was ready. My head teacher was nervous but full of expectation. The PE teacher's expression was relaxed and disdainful.

The first skill: Standing Long Jump. The full mark standard was two metres and fifty centimetres. I used eighty percent of my strength and reached two metres and eighty centimetres.

"Jumping power is not bad," PE teacher said. "What event do you practice?"

"High Jump," I said.

The second skill: Back Throw of a three kilogram Shot-Put. The full mark standard was twelve metres. The PE teacher stood ten metres behind me. I asked him to step back, he reluctantly retreated a metre. I asked him to step back more, otherwise I would not throw. He really stuck like a snail and barely moved one more metre. I asked him to move to the side more. He was like a stubborn donkey, motionless. Meanwhile, there were several students and my head teacher watching. I had witnesses to prove that I warned him. My head teacher gave me a big smile to encourage me to throw. I threw the shot put back with all my strength. I wanted the shot-put to fly longer, higher and farther. After the shot put was released, I heard the screams of the crowd. I quickly turned around and saw the PE teacher was jumping aside at least three metres and my shot put was hitting the sixteen-metre line.

The PE teacher's face was not very happy. He was not going to let me rest and announced the third test directly: Sixty-metre

Sprint. I needed to run in 7.8 seconds to finish it and I didn't know when half the people on the playground began to watch.

"How many times can I try?" I asked, not because I lacked confidence… I just didn't want to run too fast.

"Three times!" PE teacher hadn't lost his mind. I thought he would say to run as many as I wanted.

First run: I used my body engine a little bit.

"8.9 seconds," a short and powerful voice.

Second run: I was ready to end of this. I sprinted almost fifty metres with all my horsepower and left the remaining to inertia.

"7.6 seconds," a soft and hesitant voice.

Before the last item began, the school bell rang. I thought that was it, as did my head teacher. She was very happy and came to me.

"Last item, one thousand metres," PE teacher called aloud.

"Class is over," my head teacher said.

"The test is not over yet," PE teacher said. "The ten-minute break is enough to finish the test. Give up or continue."

More and more students flocked to the playground to breathe fresh air. The track was full of people. I stretched out my arm to show that I couldn't run. The PE teacher asked his colleagues to clean up the inner ring of the track.

"Within three minutes and forty seconds," the PE teacher informed. "Recess is enough time for you to run."

I hated long-distance running very much and I had never run one thousand metres before. Even if Iron Ox was here, he wouldn't want to see me run. I was going to run one thousand metres in the way I ran one thousand five hundred metres. I calculated the energy distribution. One lap was four hundred metres, so one minute twenty seconds for a lap. That was my speed for one thousand five hundred metres. At that rate, the one thousand metres was absolutely no problem. My head teacher was so excited like cheerleader. I took three minutes and sixteen seconds to finish the test. My lungs almost jumped out of my throat.

Actually, I should have gone to an ordinary high school instead of a key high school. My school never used uniform textbooks prescribed by the Ministry of Education. I was probably the only one in the whole school studying these textbooks, but even after my efforts, I could only understand sixty percent of the content. All my classmates were so goddamn smart. If the teachers were not careful, they would be criticized as fools behind their backs and would be pressured to resign. Finally, I knew what kind of person could build a spaceship or something like that in the future. I would be their bodyguard or driver. I really felt inferior, especially after examinations. Some teachers liked to rank and report scores, like the math teacher. He liked to announce the top three and the bottom three.

"Frank, ninety-eight points. You are too careless," the math teacher said. After, Frank Jr. went to the podium to get his papers. The math teacher continued.

"Only two students failed the exam," he said. "Peter, fifty-eight points. I can let you pass, but your handwriting is too sloppy. I hope you learn from this."

"Flynn," the math teacher took a deep breath and blew a gust of air. Then he kept shaking his head, and after a century of that, he said, "What's in your head? Is it paste? Nine points."

Things like that happened almost every week. There were no recreational activities in the school, except for examinations.

"Flynn, this time not bad, twenty-one points!" said the math teacher once, but his voice didn't sound encouraging.

There was another very extreme case. The physics teacher

put only five puzzling questions on the test in the hope of finding the next Isaac Newton.

"There are three students who earned zero points and only one student passed the exam in the whole grade," the physics teacher explained. "One of the zero-point students is in your class."

No surprise. It was me. I even raised my hand, curious to know who the other two were. Maybe we could help each other and improve our academic performance. As with the math, physics and chemistry teachers I had to put up with, the history, politics and geography teachers also bothered me. Because of their low status in the school, they seldom met students like me who could give them an opportunity to do their jobs.

Seven subjects flunked in the final exam of the first semester. There were only seven subjects. I made history at the school. I wasn't the only athlete enrolled in this school, but I was the only one from sports school. I was semi-professional, other guys were a quarter of athletes. The worst of them was failing in four subjects. Only such people knew how to respect me.

CHAPTER X

My senior high school had three kinds of uniforms. For winter, the puffy coat made us beavers but was not warm at all. For summer, the boys wore the same clothes as the principal, long pants coloured like eggplant that had been stored for two years and light blue short sleeves. The girls wore lovely plaid skirts and short sleeves the same colour as the boys. For spring and autumn, all wore old fashioned suits, not as old as the principal, but the colour was that of eggplant stored for five years.

There were three advantages to school uniforms:

1. They were not provided. We had to pay extra money to buy them. The school made commission.
2. There was a big gap between rich and poor students. Uniforms prevented comparison and unnecessary vanity.
3. They looked very neat.

Unfortunately, we didn't have school shoes, so everyone's eyes were on each other's feet. I began to like shoes during that period. In three years of high school, I bought all brands of sneakers except Nike. Kobe Bryant wasn't signed to Nike at that time. He signed with Adidas and was the spokesperson for the Feet You Wear-Equipment series instead. Thankfully, he only released three shoes during 1997-2000; otherwise, my mother would have severed her mother-child relationship with me.

The problem of footwear was solved. Only the problem of head was left. The school stipulated, that boys could not have long hair, and girls could not have perms. I suddenly realized that

Curly was the only person I knew who had rolling hair. My hair was very short like steel. I felt very comfortable, but I was deeply troubled by the pimples on my face. My diagnosis from the Traditional Chinese Medicine doctor: I had toxins in my body. The doctor wrote down a prescription that contained more than twenty ingredients of traditional Chinese medicine. Before my mother boiled the medicine soup for me, I checked the package of medicine and found out it contained mummified insects. I asked my mother if there was some misunderstanding. She said she didn't know, that's what the doctor gave to her. It wasn't cheap and it was troublesome to cook. Anyway, after three hours of burning gas, no matter how developed my imagination was, I couldn't think of a reason to avoid the drink. The only thing I worried about was whether I would die after drinking the stuff. It tasted so bitter. It felt like drinking freshly squeezed rubber tires. I knew Confucius' advice. *Just as bitter medicine cures sickness, so unpalatable advice benefits conduct.*

The medicine worked. I went to the toilet five times a day. The first time was hard. After, everything was diarrhoea. I was treading on air. I asked my mother if it was normal. She said it showed that I had a lot of toxins in my body and my pimples seemed to be a little bit better. That was my mother's greatest lie. I didn't see any improvement. I knew her ultimate goal was to get me to finish all the medicine she bought and not waste it. I said I probably couldn't hold on because I didn't know when I was going to have diarrhoea.

"Don't you want to be handsome?" my mother asked and paused for two seconds to see that I had no objection. "Stick to it. The doctor said you should take a course of treatment; otherwise, it will not work."

During the treatment, I wanted to sleep more in class. In

training, I ran straight out and turned to the toilet. A month later, I had lost two kilos of muscle and I might have lost two pimples.

Only a dozen students in the whole school had pimples, and none worse than me. I tried all the drugs on the market and almost turned myself into Frankenstein's monster. Nevertheless, one or two girls still liked me. Somebody even created a poem for one of them. Her name was Dan. The poem went something like this: Dan turned around for a first look and scared a cow to death; Dan turned around for a second look and scared a row of teaching buildings to collapse; Dan turned around for a third look and scared the Yangtze River to flow backwards. And Harley's satellite hit the earth and so on. There were ten sentences to describe her turning around. I didn't remember those very clearly.

I had to say that Dan was too ugly to be true. She had sesame eyes with glasses and you couldn't find her nose if there weren't two small holes in her big pie face. She had high cheekbones, two sausages for lips and a lot of freckles. Yet, despite her oil drum figure and elephant legs, her self-confidence was world-class. She even wrote me a letter. Unfortunately, it wasn't a love letter. She said my legs were in good shape, like a grasshopper. She wondered how she could have such legs.

Instead of answering her letter, I verbally replied that if she wanted legs like this, the only possible way would be to cut mine off. She didn't roll her eyes at me or scold me, she nodded calmly. She had endless questions about athletes: how to eat, how to walk, how to sleep, how to train, how to compete… And she didn't need my answers. She always solved problems by herself. She also told me how to ease the tension during competition — keep breathing deeply. I never thought about this simple thing. Deep breathing was really useful. After I established friendship with Dan, someone gave us a nickname, Beauty and the Beast.

I treated Dan as a brother. There was a law that men and women couldn't be friends. We broke the law. Dan asked me what my dream was. I didn't quite understand what dreams were. No one ever asked me such a question. I asked her what her dream was. She said that she wanted to be an environmentalist to protect the earth. She told me her dream, which made me more confused, and I told her that my mother wanted me to be a police officer. She said it was not bad to protect human beings. Dan said it would be great if I were a girl. I said she could think of me as a girl. She said it was different. She could only treat me as a friend, not a lover. Years later, I realized that she was a lesbian. But at that time, I liked her way of speaking in the clouds and mist. No girls talked to me like that except Dan. She had a heart of gold, so I wanted to remember her.

As for boys, I divided them into two categories: those scared of me and those who followed me. I developed three followers. One was my homework tutor; another lived very close to school and had a PlayStation; the last one was a pervert who stored his sperm in the fridge. He told me that masturbation was the best way to eliminate pimples. My animal instinct was awakened from his suggestion. When my body's desires were satisfied, my spirit began to struggle. About playing with myself, I felt ashamed, obscene, dirty, and despicable. I even bit myself as a warning. I asked the pervert if he had such an ideological burden. His face was a question mark and explained it was the most correct thing that human beings could do. No one would suffer pain, injury or sadness. I asked the two other followers if they masturbated. Both of them said of course not. Pervert seemed to know that would happen. He took out a newspaper called *Health Weekly*. "According to statistics," it was printed, "97% of young men masturbated..." Looking at masturbation from a scientific and rational perspective, I didn't have any doubt in the statistic at sports school, but I wasn't quite sure if this statistic held true in my high school. There were at least three hundred boys in my grade. Most of them were urban, refined, composed and honourable. They said good morning to each other and praised the good weather. No one fought and no one said rude words. They all looked white and pure like angels. I could believe in God, and I didn't want to believe that almost all of them were merely disguised as gentlemen. They were like wolves in sheep's clothing. Unfortunately, the scientific statistics were correct, and I gradually realized the hypocrisy of these guys.

One of the representative guys had named himself Space Wing, translated from his Chinese name. His English was as good as our English teacher's. He later translated the Chinese subtitles for *Inception*, the movie starring Leonardo DiCaprio, which was shown in regular cinemas, not pirated ones. *Inception eventually happened in his future; I just want to highlight his English ability.* Behind his glasses were a pair of melancholy eyes. It made you feel like he was worrying about something all the time. If there were an Asian version of Harry Potter, he would have been the best choice for Harry. To me, he was full of hypocrisy. The most annoying thing was that I couldn't find any way to give him a beating. Like when we played basketball, I deliberately fouled him. He just looked at me quietly and said, "Please be careful." Of course, I would not be more careful. I was just not very good at basketball. When I really pissed him off. He threw the ball heavily, not at me, but at the ground and left.

"What the fuck?" I shouted at him.

"I am sorry!" his expression was full of dignity.

When I walked by him, I bumped him in the shoulder. Sometimes, I slapped him hard on the back. He never retaliated.

What else could I do? Eat him like a savage? My followers thought I went a little over the top, but they understood why I was targeting him. They thought that Space Wing's girlfriend was the best-looking girl in the class. I was burning with jealousy or so everyone thought. That's why I couldn't stand it. His girlfriend's face was okay, and she looked mature for her age, but she was definitely not my type. I liked cute girls, and she had short legs and big buttocks, perfect for a pervert, not me. She was vain and narcissistic. I mean, at least twenty girls in my grade were prettier than her, even if only their faces were compared. Sometimes I just couldn't figure out where their self-confidence came from. Such people, like Space Wing and his girlfriend, even had supporters. There was a group of six arrogant females who never gave expressions of friendliness to me. Three of them had plastic surgery on their eyelids that made them look like goldfish lips. They were like Space Wing's imperial guards. When they saw me bullying him, they were a flock of birds around me ready to criticize. Then he would tell me to please pay attention next time, meaning I did hurt him. Or he would say to forget it and not stoop down to my level, meaning I needed to hurt him more.

Frank Jr. didn't like Space Wing either. He reminded me that I was caught in their trap. The more I tried to explain it in my own way, the darker it became. I should ignore them and show indifference. I found Frank Jr. was right, but he never gave me any advice. I suddenly had a revelation and pointed at him, "You're jealous of Space Wing!" Frank Jr. shrugged his shoulders to show that it didn't matter. Later, I found out that Frank Jr. was jealous of Space Wing's English ability. What a freak.

The whole school was full of students like Space Wing, they were like cockroaches everywhere. All the teachers indulged them. Whoever had good grades in school was a prince. Their wisdom was top notch. They could easily find a girl they could control. Girls could help them adjust their hormones to normal levels, so that the boys could continue concentrating on learning cultural knowledge, but these girls were the contrary. Really good girls didn't hook up with boys. None of my top ten dream girls dated any cockroaches in high school.

Let me go back to Space Wing's example and move on to high school graduation. Eventually, Space Wing was admitted to the best university in the city. His girl was admitted to the worst university in the city. They broke up when they graduated from high school. She was so upset, she even wanted to hire me to break Space Wing's leg. I didn't understand why, because I was still a virgin. She told me how deep love and hatred was, and how he deceived her affection. I thought it was okay to be cheated on. As long as she wasn't cheated on in regard to money or body, everything was negotiable. She didn't want to discuss details with me, just asked me if I would help her.

"Of course," I blurted out, and I asked her which leg to break.

"Both legs," she said. "Let him spend the second half of his life in a wheelchair."

"Do you want me to break his third leg?" I pretended to be serious.

"What's the third leg?" she asked, and suddenly realized what I had in mind. Her face burned to blush and she bit her lips, "Cut it off."

"Yes madam!" I saluted her and imagined that Space Wing's third leg must have offended her a lot.

CHAPTER XI

About four billion six hundred million years ago, Earth originated in the primitive solar nebula. The first organisms on the planet were cyanobacteria around three billion three hundred million to three hundred five hundred million years ago. These were mentioned in high school's biology class. Someone asked the teacher how the earth was formed. The teacher said that she didn't have a very clear answer to this question, and she hoped that some of the students present, would find the answer in the future. This was not a problem for me. As far as I knew, it took God six days to create the world, and the seventh day was a rest day. Another big question was where human beings came from. For me, it was also a piece of cake. God created Adam in his own image and took a rib from Adam's body and made Eve; after that, there were humans. I was very willing to accept these views, but one issue I still couldn't let go — Who created dinosaurs? Yes, dinosaurs! No one could give me a direct answer, and the Bible seemed to have lost sight of this issue. This actually meant that the problem was not very important. However, my mind was stuck on the dinosaurs who existed for fifty million years from two hundred and fifty million to two hundred million years ago. How small and impermanent I was. It would have been cool to be a dinosaur.

Since my mother started going to Church, it happened that the three religions ate at the same table. My grandparents believed in Buddhism. My aunt's husband was of the Hui nationality who should believe in Islam, though they were not very religious and all ate pork. I chose to stand on my mother's side because my father had no faith and Christians seemed to have no precepts.

There were more than ten churches in the city. What I called a church was one that could hold thousands of people. It was not a kind of cabin with a cross on it. And if you went to church on time, you would have stood across the street from the church. My mother always went an hour early to make sure she had a seat. Sometimes, she took two seats, with one for me. There were not many such incidents, especially after my father had an accident. I thought this Western God didn't have much time or energy to do things in the East.

My mother always complained about how my father put his finger into another's pie. For instance, once he caught a thief. Another time, when a bus broke down, he pushed it although he was not a passenger. When strangers fought in the street, he went to dissuade them, things like that. My mother advised him to discipline me more if he had too much time. But he seemed confident in me. He never asked me about my studies or training. He only cared about whether anyone was bullied by me. Once, I came home with panda's eyes. He gave me a slap as a greeting without asking about the cause or effect. His logic was that If I had a fight with someone and developed a panda's eye, surely my opponent was lying in the hospital. I had to say, my father was the toughest man that I had ever seen in my life. When he was younger, he was using a factory machine when he carelessly rolled his left thumb in. The nails and meat on his index finger joint were cut off. Bones could be seen. The doctor saw that my father's pectoral muscles were well developed and cut open a cross on his right chest and put his thumb into pectoral muscles, connecting the bones and flesh for two months, to later operate and dig out the thumb! Although the thumb was not very good-looking, it was at least better than a pirate captain's, otherwise he would have put a hook on his thumb.

Then came my first winter vacation in high school. I didn't remember the exact day. I finished training in the morning and went home. Nobody was at home. There was a note on the table. My mother's handwriting told me to go to my grandparents' apartment for lunch.

I saw my father in the hospital that afternoon. If I hadn't seen my mother in the ward, I wouldn't know who my father was. His head was dark purple, all shaved and two times bigger than usual. My eyes could not stay on him, and tears welled up in my eyes. I leaned against the wall and my legs trembled. I didn't know where my uncle came from. My mother asked him to help me out of the ward.

In the corridor of the hospital, I saw two police officers. They did nothing and stood there quietly. My intuition told me that they had the answers I needed, but I couldn't move a finger. I cried in silence and crouched aside like a dog. When my tears were drying up, a doctor came, and two police officers followed him into the ward. I could hear their voices but couldn't hear the content. I got up and entered the ward.

"The left side of his brain was severely damaged. His skull, eight centimetres in diameter, was smashed. After surgery, all the fragments were removed. Please, your family members need to be psychologically prepared. The survival probability is ten percent." The doctor continued, "If he survives a week, his vital signs will be stable, but he is likely to be in a vegetative state."

"So, it is impossible to know the case from the victim," one police officer stated. The other added, "The perpetrator has been caught, and regardless of the reason, he will be punished by law."

I never saw my mother cry, even at my father's funeral. Maybe it was too sudden. She was reluctant to face the reality. For my father's death, her husband's death, there was no consolation between me and her. We just kept silent.

A few months later, the suspect was eventually convicted of homicide and sentenced to life imprisonment. My uncle went to the court and heard the whole thing from the prosecutor.

The perpetrator was my father's colleague who stole copper pipes in the factory. My father caught him. The factory fired the thief, and he waited for the right moment to hammer my father over the head. After my father fell to the ground, he hammered twice more.

When I was seven years old and it was nearly summer vacation, I came home from school one day, and a homeless puppy followed me. I ran; the puppy ran. I stopped; the puppy stopped. I tried to get close to puppy; the puppy went backwards. When I reached the entrance of my building, I climbed up the stairs and looked back at puppy. Its claws touched the stairs and then it backed away, repeating several times. I turned into the corridor and disappeared from its view. The puppy began to bark. It dared not bark loud. The voice was full of despair and anxiety. I took two steps back, hid behind the wall and looked at the puppy. Puppy soon found me, and began to shake its tail and whine. I retracted my head, and Puppy barked louder than before. I put my head out again and saw Puppy stand on the first step, tail wagging like it was trying to fly. I played with Puppy for several rounds, and it almost stood on the second step. At that point, a goddamn neighbour passed by and kicked Puppy. Although the kick wasn't very hard, the puppy still landed ass first.

"What are you doing!" I shouted.

"What was it that scared me?"

"That's a dog!"

"Oh, you should tie it to a rope," the goddamn neighbour said without any regret.

I decided to keep Puppy, but I didn't realize that my mother's opposition was like seeing a tiger. She wouldn't let me bring Puppy into the house. I protested by hunger strike. That was the last thing my mother could bear. She often quarrelled with my father on the topic that my father didn't cook breakfast for me.

"You eat first," my mother said. "When your father comes back, we'll let him decide whether to keep this dog for you."

As soon as my father came in, my mother said in an unhappy tone before I had a chance, "Your son wants a dog."

"Go and buy it tomorrow!" he responded.

"Oh, yeah!" I clenched my fist and turned to the toilet to carry the puppy out.

"What? Do you agree with your son to keep a dog? The apartment is so small. Where will a dog live?" my mother continued with questions. "Does the dog have parasites? Who will serve it?"

"Put the dog back in the toilet and bathe it after dinner," my father said decidedly.

"Yes, sir!" I said.

"Give Puppy something to eat first."

"Nothing for the dog to eat!" my mother said.

"Give it some rice to eat," my father said.

I filled a bowl of rice and mixed some fish soup; I also took a carrot and a green vegetable.

"Don't waste vegetables!" my mother said. "Your teacher told you dogs eat carrots?"

"Puppy eats everything when it is hungry," I said.

"Close the toilet door and let it eat," my father said.

"Wash your hands and finish your meal," my mother said.

I finished my meal as fast as I could and crept to the toilet. I opened the door a crack. I saw that the rice was the same as before and Puppy was eating the carrot. I was quite excited to see the scene and told my parents. My mother didn't believe my message. She put down her plate.

"See? Seeing is believing," I said.

"This little thing is funny," my mother laughed dryly.

"Eating carrots?" my father asked.

"And almost finished," my mother said. "I will bring back some meat with bones tomorrow."

The shower was a nightmare to Puppy. My father almost drowned it or peeled its skin off. After the bath, Puppy shook its hair and shivered all over.

"Dry it with a towel," my father's mission was accomplished.

I named the puppy Tail, because it liked to follow behind me like a tail, and it liked to wag its tail constantly.

My father made a kennel in a cardboard box for Tail. When he pointed to Tail and then the kennel, Tail went into the cardboard box and laid down. Tail got my mother's approval. She thought the dog knew human nature well. Tail was likable. She also used Tail to teach me. She said that even a dog knew carrots were a good thing, and if I didn't eat vegetables, I was inferior to a dog.

Eating carrots became Tail's special talent and it always chose to lie in an unobstructed place and walk as close to the edge as possible. When Tail was thirsty, it kicked the water bowl twice. If nobody noticed it, Tail would howl in a low voice. Two meals a day were served on time. Tail's growth rate was amazing. In less than half a year, I couldn't hold Tail. Its front paws could be placed on my shoulders. Up and down the stairs, Tail still followed me. As soon as Tail came out of the building, he dragged me around. It was more like the dog was walking the human. On several occasions, I tried to ride Tail. I never completely pressed on Tail. It was a kind of thing when I pretended to ride on Tail and my legs would follow, but I never succeeded. Every time I tried; Tail would lie down.

Tail and I were together for two years. Because of a move, my mother convinced me to leave Tail at my neighbour's apartment while we waited for the new apartment. After we settled down, we'd pick up Tail. I believed my mother. After the move, I never saw Tail again. I had no memory of saying goodbye to Tail, not even a photo. I couldn't forget that his watery eyes were always full of expectation.

CHAPTER XII

Flowers are similar year by year. People are different as time goes by. After the first year of senior high school, I felt mature. I became a little bit reluctant to talk to others. I didn't have a common language with my classmates. They were all bookworms to me. They didn't care how short-sighted they were, how overweight or skinny they were. They only cared about their grades. In their eyes, I was a simple-minded jock. I was equally reluctant to talk to the athletes. Although they were in good shape, their brains functioned too slowly. I could feel myself loosing brain cells when I talked with them. I became a very awkward being, like a duckbill in a flock of ducks.

When my second year started, I got bad news. My head teacher, the young and kind-hearted girl who taught us chemistry, was fired from the school. Ever since I succeeded in challenging my PE teacher to skip the PE lesson, she began to give me remedial lessons. Through her efforts, the periodic table of elements was engraved in my mind like the faces of my family members. There was no time for me to thank her. She just disappeared, without even leaving a phone number.

The new head teacher was a biology major. She was just invisible; nobody took her seriously. One month later, in her biology class, she gave us a speech.

"After this period of observation, I've found that Flynn is not the black sheep of your class. Even without him, the average score of the class is still the lowest of the whole grade. Have a look towards the back of the class. You can see Flynn is again sleeping at his desk. But at least his behaviour is not affecting other people's study performance or lives."

Then, she named more than half of my classmates.

"In school, all students are equal. None of you are more special than anyone else. Your success is determined by your effort. I'm using my biology lesson to talk about this, because I know you are all geniuses here. Passing the biology exam is as easy as pie for you. I won't take up your after-school time. It's your private time, the time for you to develop yourself," she said. "With two years left in high school, it's going to flash by in the blink of an eye. These high school years will determine what kind of university you go to and will determine your future."

Frank Jr. hit me in the side while I was still sleeping at my desk. I said I was listening.

Our biology teacher's name was Jane. At the parents meeting, Jane asked my mother privately what she thought of my studying. My mother spoke about my family's tragedy. She emphasized that she had been responsible for my food and clothing, and my father used to be in charge of my education, including the decision to go to the sports school. That's the reason why my grades were dreadful, and why I had a bad temper and often argued with her. My mother really had no method to manage or motivate me. She hoped the teacher would pay attention to me, so she painted a bad picture of me.

Jane expressed understanding and sympathy. She said it was unfortunate to have a son like me and she would pay more attention to me.

Since then, Jane started targeting me. Once, I was sleeping in a math lesson, she rushed into the classroom and announced, "Your mother was laid off. Your family situation is so difficult.

Can't you study hard and let her live a good life?" She didn't say my name, but I felt that more than a hundred eyes were on me. I wanted to find a hole to crawl into to disappear. Frank Jr. was cooperative. He tilted his head and looked at me sideways. He said in a scornful tone that I should listen to Jane. I really wanted to punch his pale face, make his face bleed a little, add some healthy colour.

That day, I wasn't the only one named by Jane. She seemed to be in a bad mood. Her tone was still gentle and calm, but her face was very serious. She cursed all the girls who had fallen in love because their grades had fallen. No dirty words came out of her mouth. I liked her acrimonious way of expressing herself. Two or three of the girls cried bitter tears. The atmosphere in the whole classroom was as heavy as a funeral.

After Jane left, someone said that she had taken the wrong pill; someone said that her head had been clipped by the door; someone said that she was on her period; someone found out the truth: Jane's son had been hospitalized again.

I remember a time when Jane was in a good mood. Everyone was in a PE lesson. I was asleep on my desk in the classroom. Jane patted me on the head lightly. I was yawning and looking up, and immediately swallowed the yawn and almost choked when I saw her. She looked at me with a kind smile and said, "You gave my son your half health and my son give you his half wisdom. The quality of life for both of you will improve a lot."

"Make your son exercise more, eat more, and everything will be all right," I blurted out.

Jane suddenly realized something. She carefully and tentatively asked me what my father's height was. Then she asked me directly about my height.

"One hundred and eighty-six centimetres," I replied.

"Maybe I overprotected him," Jane said to herself.

"How old is your son?"

"Eleven years old."

"Wait for him to develop."

Jane looked at me thoughtfully, then asked, "Really?" She found herself a little foolish. A slightly embarrassed expression immediately took over her face. "Less sleep and more reading when you have time," said Jane.

In my second year of high school, every day was a repetition of the day before. I didn't fight with anyone. There was nothing special at all. When I was about to start my final year, I received a notice of grade failure and necessary repetition. Five thunderstorms grew in my brain. I encouraged myself to call Jane. She seemed more surprised than I was on the other end of the phone: "What? Are they trying to demote you?"

I thought, "If you're asking me, who can I ask?" Two days later, I got a call from Jane. She said that I didn't have to repeat my grade. I wonder how she persuaded the principal. Jane answered my question without waiting for me to turn my curiosity into verbal expression.

"I told the principal that if a person like you repeats, it will be a disaster for the next class," Jane clarified. "It's not helping you. It's harming you and others."

Jane was right. Making me repeat the grade would not solve any problems. It would only increase the number of problems. Maybe if I were forced to repeat the grade ten times, I would finally meet the standards of this school. At that time, Iron Ox told me that I already received a conditional offer from the best university. They might have been willing to wait for me for one year, but there was no guarantee after that. I didn't tell Jane this secret because I wasn't sure whether what Iron Ox said was true or not.

It turns out, some other person would advance, after I missed out on the opportunity to repeat. Before I got the details, Iron Ox asked me to guess who was coming back. I said, "Curly," without thinking. Iron Ox was surprised and asked if Curly had notified me. I told him that he hadn't informed me, it was just my intuition. Iron Ox said that I had good sense, and Curly, who went to an ordinary high school, had been demoted.

Curly and I hadn't been in touch for nearly two years — no phone call, no letter. I didn't even know his family had moved. When we met again, the sports school had a new stadium, and the toilets for men and women had been separated. We didn't feel any distance from each other when we met again. Not much had changed, though we were each more than ten centimetres taller.

"Going to Planet Namek to upgrade your combat effectiveness?" I joked. "Are all the eggs hairy?"

"Lusher than the forest."

"Let's go to the toilet and have a look."

"Afraid your heart can't take it," Curly said. "My eagle will eat your bird."

"Wow, now you are quite a talker."

"Nah, still far away from you," Curly said. "You are my idol."

I got the impression that Curly was as sophisticated as I was.

"So, what typhoon blew you back here?" I asked.

"I was going to die if I didn't come back," Curly said.

"I can understand that."

"You understand nothing," Curly said. "That's the last thing you can imagine. It cost blood."

Curly raised his chin. I saw a deep scar like a bolt of lightning about two centimetres long.

"Did your mother kill the person who hurt you?" I asked.

"You two, don't bullshit over there!" Iron Ox yelled. "Start your warmup!"

"Iron Ox is still so impulsive," Curly chuckled bitterly.

"He is much more civilized than before," I said.

"Oh my god, Kitty's tits are at least a D cup!" Curly's head was following Kitty's jogging figure. Then, his body automatically ran to her side. I ran up, too.

"Curly said that your tits are a D cup," I said.

"Do you guys have water in your head?" Kitty put on an arrogant look.

"Stop pretending!" Curly pointed at Kitty and told me, "Women like to be praised for their big breasts."

"Big breasts, no brain," I said and found that I didn't get Curly's point. It suddenly struck me that we were on different levels on some issues.

Usually, athletes who were not well-trained at professional sports school would be returned to their previous schools, but the situation didn't seem to fit Curly. Since I started the pentathlon, high jump had become one fifth of the training program. My one hundred metre record was not bad, about 11.3 seconds. Iron Ox was confident that I could compete with Curly.

First run: I used eighty percent of my power to reach 11.7 seconds. Curly was a shoulder slower than me. I knew he hadn't run his hardest. Iron Ox was not very happy to see us like that. He knew where my level was. He set me a speed limit.

Second run: I reached 11.5 seconds. Curly was a shoulder slower than me again. I was panting like a fish on shore. His breath was like a fish in the water. Then, Iron Ox decided to try something. He asked me to start first. He made Curly wait and then chased me.

Third run: Curly reached 10.8 second.

"Goddamn! How fast can you run?" I asked gaspingly.

"I don't know," Curly said.

"You don't know?" I said. "That's crazy. What's your fastest run so far?"

"It doesn't matter," Curly said. "What matters is how fast I can run now."

"Then why did you come back?" I asked.

"I want to study hard. I can't practice sports my whole life," Curly said.

"You said that you were going to die if you didn't come back," I pointed out. "And the scars on your chin."

Curly told me that he got the scar when someone slashed his face with spiked shoes. It was hard for me to imagine what kind of person would do such a dangerous thing. His facial expression was casual and gave me the feeling there was no need to discuss the issue any further. He shifted the subject and said that his culture lessons were terrible. In professional sports school, they only had four culture lessons a day, and nobody cared whether they went to class or not. The culture teachers often didn't appear. In regard to the training, because of the accommodation system, athletes had to train for about an hour in the morning and in the afternoon. The activity schedule was compact, and the intensity was high. It was unlike training with Iron Ox, when a single session was at least three hours. I agreed that even sheep grazing did not take so much time.

"You have matured a lot!" I said.

"Life is hard. Not like yours — studying well, going to go to university and having a secure job for life," Curly sighed.

"Bullshit! As if I study well!" I told Curly about my predicament. I cursed my classmates and teachers. Curly was deeply moved as a fellow sufferer. He put his arm around my shoulders.

"We must strive for success in the future." I told Curly the truth that I didn't even know what I wanted. Curly didn't give me any good advice either.

I heard from Iron Ox the reason why Curly came back. At the professional sports school, Curly trained well but was not good at making friends. When the first person who had trouble with him couldn't defeat him, things took a turn. A couple of people started targeting him. Curly's stubborn character was uncompromising, but he did try to avoid them as much as possible. They were still after him. When they'd get to him, they would force him to drink urine, wet his bedding, spread tiger balm on his penis, randomly slap him throughout the day. I wondered what their coach was doing. Immediately, I realized that not every coach was like Iron Ox. Curly's parents couldn't protect him effectively either. They were like distant water that couldn't quench a nearby thirst.

Curly's return was blessing for Iron Ox. In the history of our sports school, there were many athletes who were sent to professional sports schools and then they disassociated themselves from their former coaches. If the athletes won a medal by accident, the former coach never received a slice of the material rewards. So, when Curly returned, it was as though Iron Ox hit the jackpot. Taking Curly to the National Junior Track and Field Competition was the pinnacle of his coaching career. The host city was right at our doorstep. Iron Ox originally asked all of us to cheer Curly on. For some reason, though, he changed his mind and just let me go with him.

It was one of those magnificent autumn days. The air was crisp. I was in a great mood to be a spectator and watch someone else's competition. I even pretended to laugh a few times. Iron Ox booked a taxi. He was sitting in the front; I was sitting behind the driver; Curly was closing his eyes and resting his mind on my right. I saw Iron Ox's profile, stiff like a piece of cement. There wasn't any conversation along the way until we arrived at the stadium. Curly was the first to open his mouth. He asked me to warm up with him. Two seconds later, Iron Ox ordered me to warm up with Curly and asked me if I heard him. I said my ears still worked on my Egg Head. Curly smirked and began to recite the poem about my nick name. Iron Ox wasn't very happy with my response. He warned me not to talk nonsense any more so Curly would take the competition seriously.

Iron Ox and I followed Curly to the warm up venue. Although I wasn't there to compete, the athletes in my field of vision gave me a strong sense of oppression. Iron Ox was ten times more nervous than me.

"Are you nervous?" I asked Curly. "Deep breaths help relieve tension."

"Thank you very much." There was no trace of gratitude in Curly's voice.

Fortunately, I was not the kind of person who would quibble over everything. I thought I should remain calm for Curly's sake. I felt like I was doing something great, selfless, and unappreciated. That was my dedication.

"Oh, look, isn't this our black prince?" a voice came from behind me, and then three big guys surrounded us. My intuition told me that they were the bastards who bullied Curly.

"Holy moly!" I suddenly screamed. The bastards were shocked. I stared at them one by one, in terms of height and weight. I couldn't lose.

"Who are these morons?" I spat out. "Curly, please don't tell me that they were your former teammates. Otherwise, I will cry for you."

"What are you doing?" Iron Ox came over.

I didn't expect Iron Ox to get into his role so soon. I hadn't finished what I wanted to say yet. Meanwhile, Curly's former professional sports school coach appeared. I recognized his monkey face.

"Thank God, I finally found you!" Monkey Face put his hand on Curly's shoulder, and they walked away together.

I looked at Iron Ox. There was an awkward smile on his face. He lit a cigarette and took a deep breath. Monkey Face was a high-level coach. He treated Iron Ox like air, but I didn't give a goddamn shit about Monkey Face. He was not my coach. I was also not a grass-roots coach. I didn't need to respect him. I was nobody to him; he was nobody to me. I interrupted their private conversation.

"Who are you?" Monkey Face asked me in great surprise.

"I am his brother," I said.

"Even if you were his father, how could you interrupt our conversation?" Monkey Face asked.

"He'll tell me everything that you tell him," I said. "So, it doesn't matter whether I'm here now or not."

Monkey Face looked at Curly who was expressionless. That was an answer.

"Think about it," Monkey Face left.

"Think about what?" I lowered my voice.

"He asked me not to compete for the championship in the final," Curly said.

"What?"

"He'll pay me five thousand Yuan in return."

"What the hell!" I was shocked. "You won't do it, will you?"

"That's the same amount as my mother's severance pay for a full year," Curly said. "What's the championship worth?"

"Oh shit, you have to wait! I have to tell Iron Ox."

"Do whatever you want."

After Iron Ox listened to me, he was uncharacteristically calm. He asked me to accompany Curly. He said he would come back quickly. I had an ominous feeling that he would assassinate Monkey Face.

Curly came first in the preliminary race with great ease. I saw Monkey Face on the field and the three morons who also entered the second round, but I didn't see Iron Ox. I was sweating for Curly. But he didn't make a full sprint in the last ten metres. After the second round, Curly would enter the final ranked number two.

The one hundred metres final would be at three p.m. Of the three morons, two were eliminated. The remaining moron entered the final ranked number one.

At lunchtime, Iron Ox came back. He must have been confident that Curly would be in the final. He took us to a good restaurant. After he ordered some dishes, he took out a wad of money and asked me to count it.

"Six thousand Yuan," I announced.

"You do your best to win the championship this afternoon," Iron Ox looked Curly straight in the eyes.

Curly said nothing.

"I keep the money in Egg Head's custody. That's your reward," Iron Ox said. "I mean what I say. I'm not lying to you."

"Yes, Monkey Face is not trustworthy!" I said.

"If you try your best and you still don't win, you won't lose anything," Iron Ox resumed. "But if…"

"Yes, that's right!" I interrupted again. "If you win, you'll get six thousand Yuan. If you lose, you will see whether Monkey Face is a liar or not."

"But if you don't try as hard as you can, you will miss a chance to prove yourself. You will regret it in the future," Iron Ox said.

Throughout the lunch, Curly remained silent. Iron Ox didn't speak to him either; he kept talking to me. He asked me how my studying was going. I said like shit. He reminded me that the College Entrance Examination would be held in the second half of the semester. Time was running out. I asked him if it was true that I had a two hundred score bonus, because my head teacher said I only had a bonus score of twenty. Iron Ox told me not listen to that nonsense. A score of two hundred was a score of two hundred, no more, no less. I told him if I still couldn't get into college after the bonus marks, I would probably kill myself with cheesecake. Iron Ox admitted that I was the bullshit champion. I took his sarcasm as praise and nodded happily.

After lunch, Iron Ox put the money in my backpack. I carried the backpack on my chest and swore the backpack would be safe as long as I had breath. I told Curly that if he won the championship, I would take five percent commission. Curly said no problem. The arrangement reassured Iron Ox.

One hour before the one hundred metres final, Iron Ox took my backpack and asked me to warm up with Curly.

"What's on your mind?" I asked Curly when we were jogging.

"Nothing."

"That's impossible."

"Just keep quiet, please."

I didn't know what Curly was thinking. I saw his eyes were very firm and proud. He exuded the attitude like a king. That afternoon, he broke the national juvenile record for the one hundred metres —10.5 seconds. As he crossed the finish line, he clenched his fists, spread his arms, and roared at the sky like a beast.

CHAPTER XIII

After Curly won the championship, Iron Ox didn't live up to his promise of the bonus. He told Curly to call his parents for the money. He couldn't give it to Curly directly. I suggested for Curly to get Sissi to take the money because Frank was more face conscious. Curly said nothing. He was silent. I was really worried that he had depression.

Some days later, Frank came to see Iron Ox. I was very glad to see him. I joined them in the conversation, but no one mentioned money. My commission had gone down the drain. I heard from them that Curly was in the eye of the coach of the national sprint team. He was going to be an athlete for the China national team. However, no one was very excited about it, even though Curly's coach could be the greatest sprinter in China's history. Frank was hesitant to let Curly continue in sports. He hoped Curly would go to college. For Iron Ox, sending an athlete to the national team under his name would boost his career, and he could become a coach at the same level as Monkey Face. So, the agreement between Frank and Iron Ox was that if Curly's sports career ended, Curly would enter police college. They needed fast running humans.

Curly had come back but left less than three months later. No celebrations were held for him. No goodbye party for him, at least not anything I was invited to attend. Actually, I didn't have time to meddle in other people's business. I made a wrong decision and pushed myself into a dilemma, like a mud

Bodhisattva crossing the river, who couldn't save himself.

The college entrance examination required the completion of three fixed subjects and one optional subject. The three plus one determined your life. If you failed in the college entrance examination, you could, in theory, choose to take it again next year. But no regular high school would let you study there because the fixed high school system could not be disrupted.

Chinese, Mathematics and English were three fixed subjects. Physics, Chemistry, History, Politics, Biology, Geography, were optional subjects; students had to choose one of the six. I chose physics because there was a slogan in school: *if you are a man, you should choose physics.* Mathematics was a compulsory subject; I had no choice. I chose physics for two reasons: one was that I was a man, and the other was that I had a two hundred score bonus. I tried to figure out the math of my situation. The total score of four subjects was six hundred. The minimum entrance score for my target university was four hundred and eighty, so I needed a score of two hundred and eighty. My Chinese score was about ninety; my English score was about eighty, and my Mathematics score was about sixty. Although I hardly knew anything about physics, I only needed a score of fifty in physics out of a possible one hundred and fifty. All subject exam questions had the same composition: fundamental questions for fifty percent, moderately difficult questions for thirty percent, difficult questions for twenty percent. Even a fool who chose to be a man would choose physics. Of the whole grade, eighty percent of boys chose physics and twenty percent of girls came to join in on the fun.

After half a semester of senior year, I slowly realized how wrong my decision was. The physics teacher only analysed the most difficult questions in class. No teacher was willing to teach me the basics. I wished I could return to sports school and listen to the teacher with all the morons. At that moment, I would have to learn myself. It was very inefficient. I could easily earn a fifty score from the other five optional subjects, but I was murdered by that physics slogan. I hated slogans that always led people in the wrong direction, like the TV advertisement that said, "If you love her, give her a diamond. The diamond represents your heart." What bullshit. How could the hardest stone represent the softest heart?

Maybe I was spoiled, so I felt like physics was torturing me. In fact, compared with gifted students, my study life was very healthy.

That year, I did not miss a single game of the NBA finals, which started one month before the college entrance exam. Two of my favourite teams played each other, the Indiana Pacers and Los Angeles Lakers. Actually, I didn't really care about the two teams; I just cared about two players, Indiana's Reggie Miller and LA's Kobe Bryant. Although I bought a lot of shoes endorsed by Kobe Bryant, my favourite player was Reggie Miller. I was really enthralled by his three-point shooting. He was unlike Kobe Bryant, whom even retired aunts knew of in China. He was not popular at all. I didn't really like the same things as other people. I hoped I could find shoes endorsed by Reggie Miller. Even if they were a pair of flip-flops, I would have worn them to school.

Due to the time difference between China and America, nine to five workers and students didn't have a chance to watch the NBA Finals live. So, I skipped several morning classes. I just spent some time at home with my mother who had been laid off. After two or three games, she found out that the shoes on my feet looked like Kobe Bryant's shoes and she said that Kobe Bryant looked like Curly. Her discovery made me think she had a good eye, so I praised her. She was very happy to say that she was naturally very observant. When she was a child, she was good at learning; she was not a fool, even though no one wanted to learn during that period, so… I asked her to shut up and let me concentrate on the game.

I always wondered if Kobe Bryant or other NBA players could break the world record in high jump if they practiced. Their bouncing power was amazing.

By this time, I was a legally recognized adult — eighteen years old — and my developed bouncing power was not bad. My best performance in high jump was one hundred and ninety-eight centimetres. Just two centimetres more, and I could reach the national standard of a first-class track and field athlete. That meant I could go straight to the University I wanted to go to without taking the entrance exam. It was a pity that real life didn't end up as perfect as the fairy tales. Even worse, I sprained my ankle while playing basketball.

A few days later, Iron Ox told me that the first-class university which had planned to enrol me no longer needed me. He said there were several second-class universities to choose from and one of them would give me a full scholarship. He asked me to think about it. The news came so suddenly, so out of the blue, that I couldn't accept the result for a while. My heart was bleeding, and I dared not tell my mother, because her nagging would drive me crazy.

Some more days passed. I heard that the first-class university had recruited another athlete in the sports school who was only qualified for those second-class universities. I limped to see him. I knew he respected and feared me because I had always beaten him in competitions, and my high school was the best, while his was the worst.

The truth was more basic than I expected. The athlete's mother talked to her son's coach, hoping to get her son into the first-class university. She was willing to pay fifty thousand Yuan. The coach talked to Iron Ox. If Iron Ox allowed it, he would get thirty thousand Yuan. Faced with financial temptation and armed with the excuse of my injury, Iron Ox convinced himself to do it. He told the first-class university that my ankle was injured and whether I could recover completely in the future was a puzzle. Then he recommended the other athlete and said favourable things about him.

I couldn't believe that such a thing happened to me. The God of Fate seemed to have his plans, though. Frank inexplicably arrived at the stadium when the university enrolment list was almost locked in. I didn't meet him that day, but I know what he did for me. When he heard about my situation from Iron Ox, he was very angry. He knew it was Iron Ox who played a trick. Frank threatened Iron Ox. He would not be the recommended coach for Curly on the national team unless I was admitted to a first-class university.

The very next day, Iron Ox called me. The first thing he said was that I should thank Curly's father. Then he gave me an alternative — Medical University or Law University — and I had one day to make my decision.

I decided to go to law university because I heard that medical university had advanced mathematics, super chemistry and mega physics. These things would kill me. Then my peers would dissect my body and sell my organs.

After I had made my decision, I still asked for my mother's opinion anyway. My mother was very happy to say that if she had two sons, one would go to the medical university to be a doctor, and the other would go to the law university to become a police officer. She had only one son, so her son should go to the law university. I looked at her with great disappointment. She knew I hated the police because her younger brother was a super arrogant police officer. She said that I should try to be a high-level policeman and be my uncle's boss in the future.

Honestly, at that time, I had no interest in law and no concept of law at all. But in law, there was no such thing as advanced mathematics — the thing that made me want to commit suicide —and I didn't want to go to a second-class university. That was my logic; it seemed like my mother's.

My head teacher in senior year was a male math teacher. He was a boxing fan and he looked like a tank. When he couldn't answer the students' questions, he liked to lick his index finger secretly and sniff under his nose. Then he knew the answer magically, thanks to his mysterious ritual.

Before taking the college entrance examination, all students had to fill in their entrance voluntary forms. We could indicate twelve universities on the form. It was a total waste of time. Each had to fill in four first-class universities, four second-class universities and four third-class universities. The top first-class university was our real wish and the top second-class university was the backup plan when broken hearted. The remaining ten universities were like spectator companions of the two universities, lest they feel lonely on the form.

I filled my form with four first-class universities. I didn't fill in the rest. This was the first time I was placed first in my class. Perhaps I was the first person in our school to finish the written assignments. I handed the form to Tank Boxer. He licked his index finger and sniffed it under his nose.

"East China Law University," Tank Boxer read and looked at me. "One of the two best law universities in the country, also the best in this city."

Tank Boxer slowed down his reading speed, probably because there wasn't much to keep him reading. I stood beside the podium and looked at all my classmates. Everyone knew that below the law university, I entered the top three first-class universities in the country. Tank Boxer's nostrils flared, and he exhaled loudly. His head bounced back and almost hit the blackboard.

I couldn't tell people the truth, because they were only willing to believe what they wanted to believe. I yawned deeply and sneezed twice in a row.

"I don't think you are awake," Tank Boxer said. "If you only fill out the third-class universities, I can give you some encouragement, but you would still need a miracle."

Tank Boxer licked his index finger and sniffed it under his nose in front of me again. Out of curiosity, I did the same thing. Sure enough, it was only the strange smell of saliva.

"And what you're doing now makes me speechless," Tank boxer said. "I don't want to give up on you like that. Are there any good suggestions from the students present?"

My classmates thought the same thing as Tank Boxer, but their expressions were more restrained. Of course, there were two or three more straightforward teens, and they didn't hide their mockery.

"No suggestions!" somebody shouted.

"That's enough," my monotonous voice and expressionless face responded to Tank Boxer's ceaselessly shaking head. He directed his sarcasm towards me, but I had been steelmaking for a hundred years, so I didn't care about his words at all.

Actually, I had violated Iron Ox's request. He asked me only to fill in the law university. I added three better universities to reduce the visual impact. My achievements in the college entrance examination would be very poor if I did not pass any university admission score line. But if I filled in the names of the second and third-class universities, when they found out that I had a two-hundred-point bonus, they might lock me in before the law university. Therefore, I would not give them this opportunity. Of the other three first-class universities, if they were interested in me, I would happily be chosen by them, but that was a daydream. So, I was not playing it cool. At that time, training was put on hold. The next step was to wait for the exam, and then wait for the score.

After the university entrance examination, if I wanted to know the results prior to publication, I could know by calling a specific exam results hotline at midnight on a specific day. The telephone charges were ten times higher than a normal phone call, but that was okay for me. I would have called even if they charged me more than ten times ten.

It took almost half of my life to get through to the hotline. Following the voice prompt, I pressed my exam number with shivering fingers. I heard a robotic female voice reading my score. My breath was short and my heart was beating down my throat. I heard the robot: ... *Physical Adjustment Points: Four points. Total Score: Two hundred and eighty-two points, Please Press one to listen again. Please hang up after listening.*

I repeatedly pressed one to confirm my score, and I figured out why I got four extra points in physics, because my physics was so poor that it affected the average score of the whole city. This was the officially adjusted score.

"Hi, Mom," I called very feebly.

My mother woke up from her sleep.

"I passed," I informed her calmly.

"Jesus Christ!" my mother said. "I knew you would pass. I prayed for you every day!"

"Thanks Mom." I didn't know why tears began to form around my eyes. I opened my eyes wide to hold the tears.

The next day, I went to the stadium to tell Iron Ox the result. He asked what I did in high school for three years. It would have been better to stay in sports school. He also called over the athlete who bought my first-class university's ticket. That bastard was more than twenty points ahead of me. But I didn't give a shit, because I knew the bastard chose geography.

"The subject I chose was physics," I announced proudly. "If you are a man, you should choose physics."

"Don't listen to his bullshit," Iron Ox put his hand on bastard's shoulder. "Defeat Egg Head again in the college track and field competitions and shut him up completely."

CHAPTER XIV

To celebrate my admission to college, my mother bought me a Lenovo computer and the operating system was Windows 98. I used the modem to connect to the internet. It sounded like a tone-deaf person playing the violin. Mostly I used it to message girls online. During our chat, I created corny poems to test the IQ on the other side of the screen. Something like:

The night is wrapped in the cloak of lonesome, moonlight fell on the silent river, the distance between you and me is so close and so far, I envy the breeze, it can blow your wind bell, I want to be a stream running through your heart. And so on.

When the girl across the screen showed she admired me, I stopped talking to her. I only talked to the girls who could see through the bullshit.

I asked my mother to buy me a Motorola mobile phone when she was in a good mood. The phony reason was that I had to live in university, so she could contact me any time. The university was only three kilometres away from my home. The real reason was to make it easier for me to meet with girls I met online. The first girl I went to meet, I saw her, she didn't see me, and I ran away because she looked like a prostitute. My mother preached that my reaction was impolite. Before the second time meeting a girl, we chatted happily online, and I learned to be smart. I wrote a poem about stargazing, implying I wanted to see her picture. She agreed. I invited my mother to enjoy this picture. She looked at it carefully and only commented that the girl was fair-skinned.

I asked my mother if it was possible that the girl was testing me and sent me an ugly picture. My mother said she didn't know, but it was possible. I wondered who was more afraid? She couldn't eat me. The same as my first experience, I saw her and she didn't see me. I wanted to run away because the picture didn't deceive me. But I thought of my mother's advice and chatted with the girl for about an hour. I realized she was not very interesting in the real world. It turned out that most of the times when I thought the girl would be interesting, it was all a result of my own wishful thinking. I set a limit for myself — not to try anything more than three times. I could only meet one last girl.

The summer before I went to university, I still trained with Iron Ox every day. I became a live advertisement for him, motivation for the team members to train well and go to university in the future like me. My ankle had completely healed, and I could dunk a little bit easier than before. I wasn't too obsessed with basketball though. Iron Ox reminded me that I was not a basketball player and my event changed from teenagers' pentathlon to adults' decathlon.

I had five more items to practice, and all the sports equipment advanced to the Olympic standard. My body was more tired than before, but my mind was relaxed. Although I still had no idea what I would do in the future, I was sure that the worst thing was becoming a policeman.

My family started to regard me differently around that time. My mother had two brothers and two sisters, and my father had two brothers and one sister. There were eleven children from these eight families, because someone violated Family Planning, and someone had twins. Of the entire family (older generation and younger) I was the only child who went to university. My aunts and uncles gave me some money to express their best wishes. I used the money to buy an electric bike. It was stolen in less than a week. My mother asked my police officer uncle to catch the thief. He directly gave me a ninety percent new Yamaha fuel scooter. He had never been so kind to me. I could feel a change in people's attitudes towards me, but I wasn't quite sure what had happened to cause this because I couldn't feel any change myself. Even the proud Miss Kitty, who least wanted to see me, came to ask me if I would return to training after I entered university. My answer was intentionally callous with a hint of indifference. Still, I gave her my mobile number and told her not to call me unless anything unfortunate had happened to her, like her boyfriend dumped her or her bike was stolen. Miss Kitty quickly clarified that she was single, and her mother didn't allow her to fall in love before she went to university. Iron Ox copied my number in his address book and said that I would have to go my own way in the future. Of course, he also welcomed me back when I had time. I suddenly felt the freedom of being a college student.

The sixteenth of September was my university orientation day. My mother was reluctant to believe it. She had begun to suspect that I wasn't admitted to university, because from elementary school to high school, the start date had always been the first of September. No joke — if I hadn't participated in the athletes' mobilization meeting at the Law University, I would also have doubted whether I had been admitted. They didn't even send me an admissions notice. Anyway, I got my university ID and crowded with five other athletes into a dormitory about fifteen square metres big.

The whole dorm building was like a semi-open prison. There was only one building gate that would open at five in the morning and close at eleven in the evening, after which the electricity was cut off and boys and girls had to be in their separate prisons. Just like with men's and women's toilets, we couldn't get into each other's area.

My five roommates came from Beijing, Qingdao, Hangzhou, Guangzhou and the Shanghai countryside. It was my first time to speak Mandarin regularly in normal conversation. I felt like I was abroad, and I couldn't stand being near the local peasant, who wanted so badly to speak dialect to me, but whom I could hardly understand.

For my convenience, we five didn't call each other by names. We simply added a "Little" in front of each other's cities, like Little Beijing. Because there were two people from Shanghai, I was Big Shanghai and the countryman was Little Shanghai. Little Guangzhou was a boxer. Little Hangzhou said he was a high jumper. The remaining three were footballers. They were curious about which ten disciplines were in my competition. In order to help them understand, I introduced the decathlon in my own way: the three jumps — high jump, long jump and pole vault; the three throws — shot put, discus and javelin; the three runs — the one hundred, four hundred and one thousand five hundred metres; lastly, the one hundred and ten metre hurdle. Everyone except Little Hangzhou was surprised. Little Qingdao declared the decathlon insane. I said I didn't want to do it either, but my individual skill performances were not outstanding. With the combination of skills in the decathlon, I could safely be in the top six, and that was of the utmost importance.

"Little Hangzhou, how high can you jump?" Little Beijing suddenly asked.

"One hundred and eighty-nine centimetres," Little Hangzhou spoke with great ease.

"That's as high as I jump," I said.

"What?" Little Shanghai asked Little Hangzhou, "how tall are you?"

"One hundred and eighty-seven centimetres."

"Wait!" I said. "I jumped over the height of one hundred and ninety-eight centimetres."

"What?" Little Shanghai asked me, "How tall are you?"

"One hundred and eighty-six centimetres."

"Why did the school recruit you?" Little Qingdao asked Little Hangzhou directly.

"Because I am a top three high jumper in Hangzhou," Little Hangzhou replied. Then to me said, "I don't believe you can jump one hundred and ninety-eight centimetres."

I suddenly realized that these guys and I were not in the same world. Little Guangzhou didn't participate in our dialogue. He was sitting in a corner reading a novel by himself. I couldn't imagine him as a boxer. He looked like a scholar with glasses. I approached him for a chat. The four guys behind me started arguing about whose city was the best.

"What are you reading?" I didn't want to call him Little Guangzhou. I called him "Boxing King".

"*Martin Eden*," Boxing King lifted the book in front of me.

"Jack London." I read the author's name and asked, "What kind of story is it?"

"It should be an autobiographical novel."

"Good?"

"It depends."

"Lend me it after you finish reading."

"No problem," Boxing King said. "I have other books here, if you want to read them."

"Do you have a recommendation?"

"This is one of my favourites." Boxing King pulled out a book from the shelf.

"*The Count of Monte Cristo*."

"Have you heard of it?"

"Not at all," I said. "It is very thick."

"You can try it."

I turned two pages that night and didn't read on. The names of characters in translated novels make me feel dizzy. Before that, I only read Hong Kong martial arts novels and comic books.

The novel I borrowed from Boxing King disappeared after it laid on my desk for a week. I was nervous to tell Boxing King because I had seen him in training, and I thought it would be better not to upset him. I asked the other roommates and they all looked innocent. I offered Boxing King one hundred Yuan when I saw him and apologized sincerely. He looked at me earnestly and pulled out *The Count of Monte Cristo* from the bookshelf.

"You didn't seem very interested in the novel," Boxing King said. "So, I took it back."

"Oh my God. That is a big misunderstanding!" I blurted out a lie, "I wanted to find a time when I wouldn't be disturbed and read it in one sitting."

"This book won't disappoint you," Boxing King handed me back the book.

"Let me have a look!" Little Shanghai took the book out of my hand and flipped through the pages very casually.

"Please return my book," Boxing King said.

"This book looks boring!" Little Shanghai was still flipping through the book rudely.

In the blink of an eye, Boxing King bent down and punched Little Shanghai in the stomach. My reaction was quick, too. I had already caught the falling book in my hands.

"You'd better be careful," Boxing King pointed at Little Shanghai.

"Forget it," I stood between them. "You can rest assured that I cherish books very much."

Little Shanghai recovered from the pain. He pushed me aside

and quickly kicked, aiming at Boxing King's stomach.

Boxing King dodged back and leaned to the side, and then his fist flew into Little Shanghai's stomach instead. This time I saw clearly that Boxing King didn't use all his strength. His fist was like a dragonfly touching the surface of the water. I never saw anyone fight so skilfully, though.

"Hi guys, calm down, that's enough," I said. "No one wants to get into university and then kicked out right away for fighting."

"What's wrong with him!" Little Shanghai asked, squatted on the floor.

"He was very polite and asked you to return the book to him," I said. "But you don't listen at all."

"What did I do wrong?" Little Shanghai's eyes were full of fire.

"You said this book looks boring," Boxing King said. "You know nothing about this book! You are lying with your eyes open."

"So what?" Little Shanghai said. "It's just a book!"

"You are so pathetic," Boxing King stated. "Human civilization is destroyed at the hands of people like you."

"How about you?" Little Shanghai returned. "Only barbarians beat people."

"You kicked him too," I said.

"My kick did not touch him!" Little Shanghai stared at me, "Are you from Shanghai? Why are you supporting him?"

"He is defending the truth," Boxing King said. "If you want to fight, I'm willing to give up my left hand."

"That's very fair," I said. "Let me tie up his left hand to help my compatriot in Shanghai."

"I don't want to be expelled from university," Little Shanghai said.

"Whether you're expelled or not doesn't make a difference in the world," Boxing King said.

"It looks like you're going to be the future world leader," Little Shanghai sneered.

"Stop talking nonsense," I said. "One-on-one. Hit or shut up."

"You should shut him up!" Little Shanghai said.

"Don't waste your words on such an ignorant person," Boxing King told me. "Let's go out for a drink. It's on me."

Strictly speaking, that was the first time I drank. Before that, I had only eaten that kind of chocolate with alcohol in the centre. I got drunk quickly after a thousand millilitres of beer. I had yet to develop my drinking capacity. Boxing King drank twice as much as I did. He didn't seem drunk, but he talked a lot. The expressions he used were unusual. It felt like every sentence he said was a line-up of awkwardly-connected words. His Mandarin had a strong accent, and Cantonese words would come out when he cursed. His love and obsession of literature made me feel like I would be killed if I didn't read the novel properly. I swore to him that I would spend the weekend alone at home, quietly, seriously and conscientiously reading the novel, and I did. *The Count of Monte Cristo* was amazingly fantastic. I only put it down when I needed to sleep. Originally, my intention was to give the book a contrived compliment, but I couldn't hide my appreciation in front of Boxing King.

"How could a human being write such a story," I sighed. "Maybe I don't read enough books."

"The book resonates with me as well." Boxing King handed me the *Martin·Eden*. "This one, feels different, very realistic."

That was how I started reading novels.

CHAPTER XV

The original name of my university was St. John's. It was a seminary founded in 1879 by some American priests and had nothing to do with law at the beginning. I guess if my previous life was connected with this university, I might had been an enslaved worker or even less fortunate. So, through reincarnation, God let me have the privilege of enjoying this super garden — but I'm not a landscape lover. What opened my eyes was the curriculum that was too liberal for me to imagine, a maximum of six classes a day and three days of classes in a week. I became quickly accustomed to the learning atmosphere and I could understand what all the lecturers were talking about. I finally understood why people called it the Eden of East China. The only thing I wasn't satisfied with was that seventy percent of the students were female. Most of the other men looked like sissies.

These guys and girls from all over the country were much friendlier than the locals. It was very embarrassing that I had never heard of the hometowns of the vast majority of them. I should have taken geography, so that I could communicate with them better and not hurt their sensitive self-esteem.

In order to enhance class cohesion, our counsellor took more than fifty students to watch a movie about the Anti-Japanese War in the university's multimedia room. There was warm applause and cheers when the movie reached the wonderful part, when the Chinese hero shot down the enemy bomber with an almost damaged rifle. I was shocked. After the movie, the first committee of the class was appointed by the counsellor. I accepted the role of sports commissioner passively and most of my roommates had been offered this same position in their respective classes. They regarded it as an honour. I was too embarrassed to refuse, but Boxing King did. His theory was that group value was not personal value; it was just mutual beneficial. I looked at him as though he were an alien. He didn't give me any further explanation, although my eager eyes had already arrived. He held up a textbook on Marxist political economy.

"Do you know who Marx is?" he asked me.

"Marx, Engels, Lenin, Stalin — four kings of communism," I said. "They are all Soviet."

"Marx is German," he corrected.

"You are kidding me. That's impossible," I said. "We always put their names together."

"Very good, you found the problem," he asked. "Who do you think is the enemy: Germany or Japan?"

"Japan, of course!" I said. "Germany is our friend; Volkswagen cars are all over Shanghai."

"The United States dropped two atomic bombs on Hiroshima and Nagasaki in Japan," he said. "What are your thoughts on that?"

"That's too much," I said. "Maybe one is enough."

"Why?"

"Why what?"

"Why is one enough?"

"Because I think two is too much." I asked him, "What is your opinion?"

"Which dynasty do you think is the best in the five-thousand-year history of ancient China?"

"The Tang dynasty, of course," my reaction was definitely quick, but I was surprised his mind was leaping so irregularly.

"Why?"

"Oh man, are you in a bad mood?" I inquired. "Do you want to get a drink?"

"That's a good idea."

That evening, we discussed Mayan civilization and the Millennium — with only three months remaining, whether God would again flood the world, and if so, whether we would be qualified to board Noah's ark. I added that I wanted to lose my virginity before the world was destroyed. In the end, I threw a bicycle into the river across from the university and we stood on the bank to pee, comparing whose range was farther. It was the first time I met a person that I found interesting. But no man was perfect. The closer I got to Boxing King, the more he wanted to manipulate my thoughts and actions. He pressured me to adopt his routine and habits.

We got up at half six in the morning and went jogging with our fists waving. I found that boxers really do like to wear hoodies, just like on TV and in the movies. After morning exercise, I had two boiled eggs and a glass of milk for breakfast, then ate an apple. He told me to follow him for breakfast, because breakfast was the most important of the three meals. I was free for lunch and dinner, but like most of the time, he would have interfered with my food choices.

It was not easy for me to enter this elite educational haven. I thought that the good days had begun, but instead, I unexpectedly became an ascetic. I convinced myself that I followed Boxing King because I wanted to hear him say strange things and talk about literature. Of course, there was a little fear of his fists.

After two months, I read almost all the novels he carried and bought the ones he recommended. He really liked drinking, so my drinking increased, basically on par with his. We drank more and more. Once, he was drunk and kept giggling, then crying. His heart was torn when he shouted, "Oh God, why are you torturing me like this!" Then he asked me "why" at least a hundred times and broke a piece of glass with his fist. Fortunately, there was no apparent bleeding because he took off his shirt and wrapped it around his hand. I was almost frightened into a fool by him. The very next morning, I asked him cautiously why he laughed so happily last night. He had a bigger question mark on his face than I did. It looked like he didn't remember at all.

As time went by, I found that Boxing King was not as knowledgeable as I expected. His father was a boxing coach and literary enthusiast who published several short stories in newspapers; his mother was a community health worker. I thought I understood his roots. We just grew up in different environments. I was tired of him repeating things. I began to distance myself from him in a friendly, natural way, and found other things to do. I helped a couple of guys in my class who wanted to improve their athletic abilities, because I was a respected sports commissioner, and sports accounted for five percent of scholarship evaluations. Students had to pass sports to qualify for evaluation, even if they had full marks in every other subject. All of that effort in the other courses would be useless. What was more extreme was that without passing sports, you couldn't graduate with a bachelor's degree.

For the first time, I felt the existence of sports important, but I didn't imagine anyone could actually fail. Unfortunately, I was wrong. There was a man whose sports ability was hopelessly poor. I sincerely advised him to give up. The man, from the northeast and who looked like a potato sack, stared earnestly at me. He was the cultural commissioner in my class. He put his hands together and worshipped me like a bodhisattva. I feel like there were wings on my back or a halo around my head. He said he would do anything for me, and I said I would like to take his place in the examination, but sports exams were not as easy to cheat as culture exams. He almost knelt on the ground and begged me. He said that I was a local, and the PE professor was also a local. It was easy for local people to communicate with each other. "All right, however there was no guarantee I would succeed in my scheme," I thought it over in my head and said, "I would do my best."

The communication between me and the PE professor was very local and direct. I asked him to do me a favour. He asked me to get ten points in the university track and field competitions. I said no problem. The professor gave me a mysterious smile. I felt like he knew something, but I couldn't be sure. I guaranteed him what I said was for real. He told me what he said was for real.

I let the cultural commissioner know about the deal between me and the PE professor. He asked me what the concept of ten points was. I told him that I had to come in fourth place or better in two individual events. After listening, his whole face turned waxy yellow.

"That's impossible," he told himself. "The comprehensive ranking of our school is sixth in the city and there are also sports universities."

"Relax," I said. "Come and cheer me on during the races."

He was in a trance for a moment and then swore he would go.

I regretted inviting him to cheer me on. After that day, he kept on offering me bananas, biscuits and energy drinks, and kept asking me about the time of the competition. I told him that I wouldn't miss it as long as I was alive. He said that knowing the time of the match could help me arrange the training plan. He borrowed a few sports books from the library and wanted to study with me. Before I could say anything, he blocked my mouth, explaining that he (the coach) didn't need an athletic background.

How did this situation turn upside down? Who on earth needed to improve his sports level? He was like a mosquito flying around my ear. He even got the transcript from last year's university track and field competitions! It touched me a little.

I used to compete against local people. Things changed. Athletes from other cities could also get into Shanghai's universities with extra points or references. I felt a severe challenge. My best performance in high jump could be placed third. And in long jump, I could only get sixth. That meant, last year, I would have only earned nine points. This felt a little strange to me, but I didn't think the PE professor would care too much if I only needed to improve by one point. As for decathlon, the final result was a score. I had no idea what my score was or how it was calculated, because it would be my first time to participate in the event. However, I didn't feel bad.

The competition was held on the weekend before Christmas. I had never participated in a formal track and field competition in winter. Usually, the only event held in winter was the Happy New Year Marathon, and anyone could participate.

Fortunately, it was a warm winter. The lowest temperature was about seven degrees and there was no wind. The track and field organizing committee might have thought that the weather was too good to waste. They quickly arranged a match to make the season interesting.

Unsurprisingly, Iron Ox appeared on the day of the

University Track and Field Competition. I was really happy to see him, but I pretended to be even happier. We shook hands like old friends. He said he was there to cheer me on. His voice hadn't even stopped when we became astonished by a group of people shouting refuelling slogans. They were chanting my name. The cultural commissioner organized a group of people to cheer me on! I couldn't recognize a few of the faces, they were probably his fellow townsman. I could understand that their weekends were boring, and watching a race was good entertainment. I should charge admission fees.

"You are doing terribly well," Iron Ox said. "I've never seen anyone with such a cheerleading team."

"Don't cheer when I am in the race!" I shouted at the people in the stands, "I will be distracted!"

"No worries!" the cultural commissioner shouted back. "We are a civilized audience!"

"These countrymen came out to broaden their horizons," I explained to Iron Ox, shrugging my shoulders in helplessness. "It's quite annoying."

"Don't underestimate them," Iron Ox said. "Those who can enter your university are not nobodies."

"My high school classmates were all somebody. So what?" I asked.

Iron Ox didn't refute my point of view. He said that I was telling the truth. Ultimately, people had to rely on their own strength to speak.

On the first day of the decathlon, I did a good job. In order, I completed the one hundred metres, long jump, shot put, high jump, and the four hundred metres. After those five events, my score temporarily ranked first! I felt like my body had been hollowed out. Unexpectedly, the PE Professor even had me run a four by one hundred metre relay. They were going to squeeze me dry like sugar cane. I could feel my muscles had accumulated a lot of lactic acid when I got up the next day. After the one hundred and ten metre hurdles, discus throw, pole vault, and javelin throw, I was still in first, but the gap between me and second shrank from three hundred points to a dozen points. The competition was between me and him. Whoever won the one thousand five hundred metres would be the champion. I felt very sorry this was not *Forrest Gump* or anything like that. Endurance running was my weakest event. I almost finished the race with a spacewalk, and my total score placed me nearly in third. I was upset. It felt like someone had stolen from me. I hated when we took the decathlon group photos, and directed at them, "Trash, you guys only have the same endurance as cattle." No one dared to confront my words, because to be good at endurance running was not a glorious thing.

In the end, I earned fourteen points. I wanted to borrow a wheelchair for the next week. My roommate Little Hangzhou jumped his personal height record but got nothing in the high jump competition. We all broke our university record for high jump, but the record holder could only have one name, and that was me. I also broke the record for long jump, pole vault, shot put and set the decathlon record. The PE professor fulfilled his promise and gave me a bonus of one thousand seven hundred Yuan. I never had so much money; it was awesome. As for the cultural commissioner, he already regarded me as an idol. Before the final exam of the first semester, he predicted the range of answers for essay questions in nine subjects and printed them on more than twenty A4 sheets of paper. He told me not to read the textbook — it was a waste of time — just to recite the answers on the paper. That would be enough to pass the exam. But he didn't tell me when to start reciting, so I started the day before the exam. I found out that one day of studying was not enough at all. I recited the answers very carefully and forgot them very quickly. I copied the answers on a scrap of paper in case I forgot them, wrote them as small as ants. As for the multiple-choice questions, we had specific gestures between us. Even so, I still hadn't passed one of the subjects and none of my roommates passed either. It was Ancient Law which made me feel illiterate. The archaic characters played on my limited imagination.

During the five thousand years of Cathaysia, our ancestors were a little violent. All criminals suffered varying degrees of physical torture. Authorities would have tattooed half your face, which showed everyone you were a criminal. The rest of the punishments were full of blood and absurdity. For example, if couples were disloyal, the sexual organ of betrayer would be destroyed without anaesthesia. When someone did something else wrong (I forgot the crime) they would be tied to a stick, and their body would be suspended above a big pot filled with excrement heated from the fire below.

Our philosopher professor told us, "That which is real is reasonable," from Hegel.

CHAPTER XVI

No homework, no training. The university winter vacation bored me and I hadn't had a haircut for half a year. My mother said I looked like a sissy. She gave me money to cut my hair short. While I was waiting at the barber's, I looked through some hairstyle magazines. When it was my turn, I pointed to a photo and told the barber I wanted to perm my hair wavy. After the procedure, my hair was curled like an African's. I held up the magazine and looked blankly at myself in the mirror. The barber explained that freshly permed hair was like this. After several washes, it would be exactly the same as in the photo. My mother thought I looked cute, but she was worried the university professors would criticize me. I was not in the mood to explain to her how free and openminded the university was. I told her straightaway that I would cut it short soon and put on a woollen cap.

During the vacation, I still wandered aimlessly on the internet all day long, flirting with people who showed up as females. When we needed to exchange photos, I sent my roommate's photos randomly. The photos I sent were the real people I could find. At a certain moment, I received the same photo from two different people. The girl in the photo was beautiful, and I really felt like I was falling in love with a photo. So, I chose to continue the more interesting conversation with the one who sent me the article "One Hundred Movies to Watch Before You Die". I printed it out and went to the video shop. They only had thirty percent of the movies from the article. But even just that thirty percent completely changed my understanding of movies that were not shown in the cinema here. For instance, before *Godfather I, II,* and *III*, and *Once Upon a Time in New York*, I had only seen mobster movies made in Hong Kong. The gangsters would always have bare upper bodies, ugly tattoos, no muscles, and were constantly chopping up each other. Seeing *Terminator I* and *II* left me speechless. *Braveheart* was very heroic, and I learned how hard democracy was to create; though I didn't believe the bride's virginity had to be dedicated and given to the lord. *Eyes Wide Shut* and *Pulp Fiction* were very weird. *Malèna* was a very good, educational film for boys.

During the holidays, except for eating, drinking, excreting and sleeping, I only watched movies. I spent almost all of my money on movies. I legitimately bought one movie in memory of a Hong Kong star who committed suicide by jumping from a building due to depression. The rest of the movies I bought were all pirated copies. They were one tenth the price, saving me a fortune, and the picture quality was not bad.

Later, I joined the university's film exchange society. Each member had to contribute three movies, then put them in a cloth bag and everyone randomly picked up three. After a week, members could exchange movies directly. The organizer explained it was to prevent us from picking and choosing. I thought it was a good idea and although I got two bad movies at first, there was another movie that seemed good. While I was reading the synopsis, someone tapped my shoulder twice.

"That is the movie I brought, yo," a sissy voice said. "Philadelphia! You are lucky, yo. The content of the story is about two lawyers…"

"Stop it!" I said. "I don't want to hear the details. If you want to take it back, I'll give it to you now."

"I don't mean that, yo," the sissy voice said. "I just hope you'll find the film interesting."

I looked at the guy in front of me. He was as tall as my shoulders, thin body, wearing a pair of glasses, nothing special. He shook hands with me like a girl and told me his name was Vig. Then he began to marvel how manly my hands were. He took my hand and looked at it over and over in admiration. He also touched the palm of my hand with his finger.

"Wow, you have muscles!" Vig gently pinched my arm and said. "I'm so jealous!"

I cracked my neck from side to side. Vig put his finger on his teeth and breathed in. It was like I broke his bones, or something. He asked, "Doesn't that hurt?"

"Where are your other two films?" I asked and hoped he could leave me alone.

"Um…" Vig bit his index finger and looked around. "I don't know exactly where they are."

Suddenly I had the feeling that Vig was different. The animal instinct in my body demanded that I should be nicer to him. I slapped his bum in the same way I did when messing around with my guys in sport school.

"Woah, what are you doing?" Vig's speech was slow and meek.

I looked at him with a grin on my face, as if I had discovered a new creature. I took advantage of his absentmindedness and patted his bum again. Vig stamped his foot and told me if I did that again, he would be angry. I couldn't believe my eyes, so of course I did it again. He really seemed angry and turned away. I rushed to catch him, put my hand on his shoulder and started to apologize.

"Hey, don't touch me!" Vig twisted his body. "You are so annoying."

"Is this how you always talk, your voice, your gestures?"

"Yeah. Do you have a problem with that?" Vig looked at me with innocent eyes.

"I feel sick," I pretended to make a sound of vomiting.

"Are you okay?" Vig said and genuine concern flashed across his face. "I can go with you to the hospital."

My body felt itchy, but I couldn't find the source. He didn't look like he was putting on airs. It made me feel a little overwhelmed.

From that day on, Vig's sissy voice was always nearby. While I was playing basketball, he was watching; while I was playing football, he also was watching. When I asked him how he managed to find me every time, his tone was very relaxed. He said it was not difficult to find me, since I was either on the basketball court or on the football field. That was true. Ball games were going to be my main sport; even the University team invited me.

"How can you be so feminine?" I asked him.

"Um..." He rolled his eyes from the bottom right corner to the top left corner and said, "This is my personal freedom."

"You shameless eunuch." I then asked, "Is there anything in your crotch?"

"Would you like to play volleyball?" he said, changing the subject. "There are many pretty girls with nice bodies."

"I am not interested!"

"No wonder you like hanging out with men," he said. "Because you like men."

"What eunuch logic is that!" I pointed to a group of men. "Do they all like men?"

"You never know," he said.

I suddenly realized that he was setting a trap for me. I stopped talking to him and walked away. He moaned behind me that I was impolite to leave without saying goodbye. Without turning around, I flipped him a middle finger.

After that day, things changed again. I still played basketball or football when the weather permitted. Vig, however, was no longer regularly popping up by my side. And when he did appear, there would always be several girls with him. They also played basketball, but like shit. Sometimes they jumped rope, sometimes kicked shuttlecock, sometimes ran two or three laps around the courts and did some exercise.

There were always three or four ordinary girls who appeared with Vig plus one or two random faces. I wasn't sure what the eunuch was doing. I didn't really care until one particular girl appeared. I was frightened by her brash laughter. I automatically approached them when I was taking a break in basketball rotation. I heard her call Vig "sissy" with her super decent northern accent. I was so fascinated by her voice. Vig saw my proximity as aggression. His expression was not friendly.

"What are you doing here?" he asked.

"I agree with the madam's description of you." I thought it was the best way to show my goodwill, but I didn't expect the northern girl to frown and stare at me.

She asked, "Is this yak sleepwalking and lost?"

"Wendy," Vig said proudly, "let's ignore him."

"Did the teacher stipulate, that boys should not have long hair and girls should not have perms?" Wendy directed at me. "You broke two rules at once, and I almost couldn't tell if you were a man or a woman."

I was speechless for a moment, because Wendy was the kind

of girl who could be called Miss Beauty. Her nose was narrow and straight. She had big eyes and double eyelids, a baby fat face with a sharp chin. Her small mouth looked like a cherry and she had a thick ponytail. If she had a devilish figure, she would have been perfect.

"The fashion of this city is destroyed by a peasant like you." I didn't know why I said that.

"Your city was only a small fishing village in history," Wendy said. "Your fashion is superficial."

"She comes from the capital, Beijing," Vig said.

"Shut up," I said, "Your parents should have castrated you at birth."

I was outnumbered in the war of words. I could hardly sleep that night. All I could think about was Wendy and it had absolutely nothing to do with hate. There was a strange restlessness in my body. From the next day onwards, I began to pay attention to Vig. Interestingly enough, the bastard just disappeared. I happened to meet Wendy in the canteen twice, but I avoided confronting her. I looked at her from where she could not see me. She was so cute when she laughed. My heart had special contractions and I felt my blood go straight from my heart to my stomach. I had a really good appetite that day.

It was almost ten days later when I saw Vig again. I greeted him with a smile. He looked haggard.

"Where the hell did you go?" I asked.

"Did you miss me?" he asked.

"I was dying I missed you so much!"

"Then why didn't you call me?"

"I don't have your number."

"You're a liar."

"By heaven and hell, I swear!"

"Did you see *Philadelphia*?"

"Of course, I did." I replied without thinking.

Vig bypassed me and walked away without a sound. I caught up with him. He stopped and shook like an old engine. He was weeping silently, and passers-by threw curious glances at us. I quickly pulled him aside to the garden.

"What happened?" I was a little flustered.

"I put my contact information on the movie disc!" he said. "I almost died."

"Don't exaggerate," I said. "To tell you the truth, I haven't seen that movie yet."

"I don't believe you," he said. "I really wanted you to visit me when I was in the hospital."

"Are you really a goddamn eunuch?"

"You have no heart," he sighed. "Please let me go."

I watched him run away like a soft-footed crab. I felt something was wrong. Those three exchange movies were lying in my dormitory. I opened the disc from Vig and found the note. It said, "Hi dear friend, I am very glad to participate in the movie exchange activity. I hope you can enjoy the movie and share your impressions with me. Your friend, Vig." I called the number on the paper.

"Guess who I am." I held my nose and pretended to speak in a sissy voice.

"Um, sorry, I don't know."

I continued to play with him until I lost my patience. When I spoke with my normal voice, he still couldn't guess who I was, but as soon as he heard my name, he hung up. I was instantly curious about the movie. I got on my scooter and headed home. I didn't like watching movies with other people; their reactions were always out of sync with mine. They always laughed when they shouldn't have; they didn't laugh when it was time to laugh, or the sound of their laughter was too much.

Philadelphia refreshed my worldview on life and values. I searched online about homosexuality and AIDS, and I was completely shocked, especially in regard to AIDS. There was no cure. It was easy for me to put Vig in the pathetic role. I sent him a mobile message: *Hi man, God put your soul in the wrong body. It's not your fault. I just opened your movie today, finished watching it alone. I don't know what to say. I think mankind's scientific progress should conquer virus in the near future. I'm sorry for my past behaviour. I hope everything is okay with you.*

Vig texted me that he would accept my apology, but I should invite him to Pizza Hut. I really had no appetite to eat alone with him, so I suggested eating in the canteen. Vig resumed texting that my apology was insincere. Suddenly an idea came to me. I had wanted to get together with Wendy, but I had no natural way to do so. I texted that just the two of us could not finish any of the items on the menu at Pizza Hut, half of the pizza would burst him. He replied that he had a small appetite, so he would invite Wendy, if I didn't mind. Of course, I had no objection. This was called a dream come true! I covered my joy by texting about how Wendy was a tigress, and if there were other better candidates, it was better not to invite her. I could feel the glee from Vig. He texted that he had no other candidate, and my excuse was insincere.

Our appointment at Pizza Hut was for lunch the next day. I saw Wendy was sitting by the window when I parked my scooter. Vig was late, and his voice came from behind me, as I was praying he would not show up.

"You are so punctual," Vig said. "Wow, you even ride a motorcycle."

"You look well," I said.

"Um, if someone invites you to lunch, you would be in a good mood."

I was not sure about Vig's condition. Although breathing and normal physical contact would not be a problem, I thought it was better not to touch him. Vig saw through my idea. He patted me on the shoulder and said, "You really think I have AIDS?"

"I won't discriminate against you," I said.

"Come on, I am still a virgin!" Vig said. "I was hospitalized because of heart condition."

"Really?" I asked. "Then why didn't you clarify?"

"I did it on purpose," Vig explained. "Because I knew you would react this way."

As we talked, we went into the restaurant. I sat across from Wendy, she remarked, "Well, here we are. You gained at least one brownie point."

My heart contracted again, and I could clearly feel the blood flowing to my stomach. I didn't know why I felt a little soft all over.

"Don't frighten him," Vig said. "He is outwardly strong but inwardly weak."

"I knew it," Wendy said. "Southern men are cowards."

They both had big mouths when talking but didn't have the same mouths when they ordered food. They didn't seem to be using me financially. I wasn't going to be stingy, though. I always ordered a lot of food. The two of them talked endlessly. The content of the conversation was elevated, full of proverbs and idioms. I felt illiterate. Every now and then my eyes fell on Wendy's face. Sometimes she pretended to ignore me; sometimes she stared at me and asked if there was paint on her face; sometimes she frowned to comfort me and said that life was still hopeful, and not to despair.

I finally managed to squeeze out a sentence to ask her. "Do all Beijing girls glib talk like you?" She said scornfully that Beijing was full of girls who were much better than her, that she was ordinary. I put out my lower lip as a sign that I didn't believe it. She put on a helpless look and said that she was not even average, otherwise she would be reduced to the south. Vig chimed in that he was also the same level of helpless when he came here. I had a cunning idea. I asked Vig if he was in love with Wendy, why had he asked her out to lunch, and if he wanted me to be Cupid. I was very pleased with my own counterattack, but in an instant, it collapsed. Wendy took Vig's shoulder, "We are sisters."

The sisters tried so hard to make me sick. They passed food to each other as if they loved each other. They also voted to accept me as their youngest sister. I wanted to pretend to be against it. As soon as opened my mouth, Wendy pointed at me, "That's it! You have no right to speak."

"I want to express my gratitude to you both." In order to maintain the harmony of the atmosphere, I said, "It's a great honour for me."

After lunch, Wendy wanted to try my scooter. I was sitting at the front. Vig was sticking to me and Wendy was sticking to Vig. Three persons on one scooter — it was obviously overloaded. Fortunately, we didn't get into a traffic accident and I got them to their destination safely.

I created a very serious and responsible analysis of how I felt about Wendy. I had more than favourable feelings, but less than love. I liked the way she talked, but felt sorry about her figure. I subtly told her to work out with me. She said she was already smart and had a pretty face. If she had a devilish figure, it would be chaos, and she would not have any time left to waste on me. There were always some pitfalls in her words, but I really enjoyed it.

CHAPTER XVII

I had a dream. In an indoor track and field arena, I saw Curly preparing for the final. He and his rivals were all naked. The objects between their legs swayed like pendulums as they walked. I didn't see how he finished the race. When I asked him why he was naked, he was already wearing sweatpants and said that to win a game, people need to be absolutely confident. If runners didn't care about anything, they would have the best form. Then my cell phone rang. This time the dream was fairly complete, unlike the usual, ruined before the end, what a nightmare!

It was Iron Ox calling. He recognized my sleepy voice and was surprised that I was still asleep at two o'clock in the afternoon. He told me if I needed to go back to sleep, I could call him back when I properly woke up, because he had something very important to say. I knew he was just pretending to be polite to me. He asked me if I had a pen and paper with me. It took me five seconds to sit down at my desk. I wrote down a specific time and threw the pen away. Iron Ox asked me to repeat the information which he had just told me. I repeated the time and place. "Carry spiked shoes," he stressed again.

I stretched my voice impatiently and told him not to worry. He hung up the phone. I didn't know exactly what I needed to do, and I didn't bother to ask. A minute later, Iron Ox called again. I was asked to repeat the time and place. After my precise retelling, he told me to take a taxi instead of driving a scooter. He would reimburse the fare.

I wanted Wendy to have a new understanding of me, so I invited her, and she readily agreed and informed Vig. I told Vig privately not to be a third wheel. He replied that he would take a taxi to watch some sports, and that he wouldn't miss such an opportunity. He could sit next to the driver with his eyes closed.

At the appointed time and the appointed place, after the taxi started, my regret began to sink in. First, I sat next to the driver. Second, these two guys kept talking nonsense.

"Um… If you go on like this, you will wither like autumn flowers," Vig said to Wendy.

"Unless a person is in a harmonious relationship," Wendy started, "it is better to be free and live alone."

"Um… I have good news for you," Vig lightly touched my shoulder and said, "This man likes you."

"Oh, that's bad news for me," Wendy said without hesitation.

"Who said I liked her?" I turned and asked.

"I allow you to fantasize about me in your mind," Wendy said to me. "But don't make any declaration of intention in the real world."

"It's cruel of you to treat him like that," Vig said. "The Constitution gives us the right to freedom of speech."

It suddenly dawned on me that I didn't really want to invite Wendy, let alone Vig. If Iron Ox hadn't offered a free taxi, I would have been riding my scooter.

"You see, this little man is starting to dive and stop talking," Wendy said. "You southerners are small-minded."

"It's you northerners who are too rough," taxi driver interrupted. "You can stay away from bathing for weeks."

"Is your wife from the north?" Wendy asked.

"Are you kidding me?" taxi driver scoffed. "We southerners

will not marry northerners."

"How do you know that northerners don't bathe for weeks?" Wendy asked.

"I sometimes get passengers from the north who smell so bad," he explained. "When they open their mouths, the car is full of garlic."

"Garlic smells just right and helps kill bacteria in your car," Wendy said. "I haven't disliked the smell of smoke in your car yet."

"Garlic can kill bacteria, but it should not be eaten too much," taxi driver said.

"How do you know who eats too much garlic?" Wendy asked. "Eating one or ten garlic cloves gives off almost the same smell."

The driver was a little unclear about the situation. Fortunately, his reaction was not on the same frequency as Wendy's, and he didn't mean to quarrel. He smiled and stopped talking. Wendy's emotions were coming up. She felt like she wasn't enjoying herself yet. She talked to herself about the historical and cultural differences between the North and South. Vig didn't care about Wendy's topic at all. He was totally talking to himself about whether there would be many muscular men. His imagination alone made him very excited. I had to save energy and didn't talk to them. Although I didn't know exactly what I was going to have to do, I thought it must be something strenuous.

Near Shanghai Stadium, my phone rang. Iron Ox was on the other end of the line and asked me where I was. I said I was about five minutes away. The driver heard me speak in Shanghainese, so he began to speak back in Shanghainese. This upset Wendy again. She asked us not to use alien language and to please speak

Mandarin. I told the driver in our dialect to ignore her as a fool and I spoke very fast. Wendy miraculously knew that I called her a fool. I thought she figured it out by instinct, so I just denied it. Then I went on to say that if she could understand, sows could climb trees. The driver burst into laughter and reminded me to be careful, that many northerners could understand our language. However, Wendy insisted that I scolded her as a pig. No matter how hard I tried to deny it, she didn't believe me. Then she began a long monologue that went on until we entered the stadium.

"Wow, the National Track and Field Grand Prix Final," Vig read the banner. "I heard that this is the best stadium in China nowadays. It's really spectacular!"

At that time, there were no tickets at all for the National Track and Field Grand Prix Final. It was like a free private party and the host didn't invite any guests. Whoever came was a guest. I took them straight through the bleachers to the stadium and I warned them not to wander around the infield. They were both highly educated and kept following me, but twittering like two birds. At about the same time, Iron Ox and I saw each other. He was in the high jump area and waved to me. I jogged toward him. Vig hurried to ask me where I was going. I ignored him.

After I met Iron Ox, he looked me up and down. He asked me if I had practiced the high jump recently. I falsely claimed to have practiced two or three times. I had actually played basketball or football every day, so he didn't see anything wrong with my shape. He pulled out a sports vest and shorts of his bag which looked like rags. I told him I had gear. Then, he began to tell me what I needed to do.

I was going to take the place of a man named Luther to reach the national secondary track and field standard. I needed to jump over one hundred and eighty-three centimetres. But because this was the finals of the National Track and Field Grand Prix, the contestants in all events were among the top eight in the country. Iron Ox told me that the lowest take-off height was one hundred and eighty-five centimetres and I was the only one to take the test. He told me to abstain once I succeeded in the jump, and talked about Luther had once jumped one hundred and eighty-three centimetres, but unfortunately his records passed the expiration date. The university he was going to enter required a valid certificate, but he happened to sprain his ankle playing basketball, just like me.

I wasn't interested in Luther's pathetic story. I told Iron Ox, and he also knew, that I had never tried more than one hundred and seventy-five centimetres as a take-off height. If I was out of form, I might have stopped at one hundred and eighty-five centimetres. He said he knew, and he had faith in me. To be honest, I was in amazing form that day. I ran and jumped in the field, stretched and warmed up my body.

My two guests couldn't figure out what I was going to do. Vig was so excited that kept making a lot of noise. Wendy was very restrained. Her whole face seemed to be covered with styling glue.

Because I was the only one who started jumping from the lowest height, Iron Ox asked me to measure the footstep position and jump over the cross bar stealthily. I was wearing sweatpants and flying across the bar very elegantly. A referee warned me not to cross the bar again before the game began. Another female referee smiled and said that I was in good shape to break two metres. I saw her every year when I took part in municipal competitions, but I didn't expect that she should remember me. Iron Ox saw it, too. He told me to ignore her.

The competition officially began. I wore the sports vest and shorts. Vig was thrilled again. I turned my head and glared at him. He rushed his finger into his mouth. I glanced at Wendy, her brows wrinkled like a creek and she looked at me intently. I took a deep breath, raised my hand to signal that I was ready to jump, and the referee waved the flag. I ran up and used the Fosbury flop over the bar. Job done. When I was about to leave the sponge pad, I hesitated for a second. Then I held my ankle and pretended to be injured. I slowly moved my body out of the way and limped to the referee. I announced to them that I had to withdraw from the event. The female referee felt sorry for me. She repeated that my form was so good. Iron Ox didn't care about my acting. He arranged for me to finish in such place. He knew no one would really care.

After I quit the competition, the bar went straight up to two metres. I wasn't in the mood to watch the event. Iron Ox gave me one hundred Yuan as taxi fare. I told Vig to shut up before he said anything. Wendy's face was full of concern and asked me about my injury. I told her it was okay. I didn't know why my mood suddenly became worse. I left directly. That afternoon, in the men's one hundred metre final, Curly won his first national championship. I wasn't able to witness the moment. I got completely drunk after I saw the news. I hadn't contacted him for almost a year, and I missed the final right in front of me. I felt like I didn't know myself. There was an unusual sense of loneliness surging from my heart and then my tears flowed down.

I was the kind of person who woke up and was okay with everything. I called Curly and blamed him. Why he hadn't contacted me for so long? He explained it like he was in the wrong, that he trained like a dog every day, and didn't even have time or energy to have a girlfriend. He told me that every Thursday was his day off and I could visit him in the countryside and stay for a night if I was interested. I thought I should strike while the iron was hot. We agreed to meet on the upcoming Thursday. Before hanging up, he asked me to bring some adult movies. I felt like his life must really be boring. But I didn't know what his preferences were: fresh or heavy; Japanese or American; animation or animal. Fortunately, the entire male dormitory building was the International Adult Film Free Exchange Centre. The spirit of sharing was the most selfless aspect of human beings. I visited only two dorms and filled up my hard drive.

On the day I went, I took the subway for an hour, then took a bus and walked for another hour. On the way, I called Curly to start moving his ass to pick me up. At a crossroads, I decided which way to go. After a few steps, I heard a familiar voice behind me.

"Egg head, Egg head, no worries about the rain, People have umbrellas, I have Egg Head." Curly rode his bicycle slowly and shouted, "Stupid! Wrong direction!"

"I want to buy a bottle of water at the supermarket over there," I said. "You could have picked me up from the bus stop with your goddamn bike?"

"It is broken," Curly shook the back seat. "Walking a few steps will not kill you."

"You could also have come to the bus stop," I complained. "I'm like a headless fly."

"Stop!" Curly said. "You'll get to eat a big meal to reenergize in the evening."

"You seem goddamn taller! Get off your bike," I demanded. "Let me check."

"No need to check," Curly said. "Three centimetres taller than you."

"One hundred and eighty-nine?" I asked. "How is that

possible?"

Curly showed an air of elation and satisfaction. His bicycle was riding like the Arabic numeral "8". I followed Curly to his dormitory; his room was as big as my dorm, but there were only two single beds. There was even a balcony. Outside the window was a piece of green. I could see the red track through the leaves. It felt isolated, very quiet with only bird calls.

All afternoon, we played PlayStation. Curly chose China to kick my Brazilian team three to nil. Then he chose France, Italy, and Argentina. He crushed me completely. I didn't care much about those childish things, though. It made me feel happy to see him as a happy fool.

At dinner time, Curly asked me to wait for him in the room and if another knocked at the door, to ignore it no matter who it was, because I was not allowed to be here. I wasn't nervous at all. I even showed contempt and told Curly that I was hungry. Twenty minutes later, someone knocked at the door. For safety's sake, I didn't make any noise. Then I heard the key inserting into the lock, Curly came back. He put two stainless steel bowls full of food on the table: pomfret, soft shelled turtle, lake shrimp, beef, and some vegetables.

"Where is the rice?" I asked.

"How can you go hungry with so much food?" Curly asked.

"My mood won't be stable without rice," I said.

"You are farmer!" Curly said. "There's a mouthful of rice under the food."

This was one of my happiest diets. I felt like a mouse in a food bucket. Curly apologized without sincerity that this was the maximum food he could cram in. I motioned to him to shut up with a wave of my hand.

Curly had nothing to do and began to test the adult movies.

"What the hell is this!" Curly shouted. I glanced round and saw a white man entering a chicken.

"What's the matter with this woman!" Curly fast-forwarded the movie and said loudly, "Have you noticed the moans of the Little Japanese are so fake?"

My mouth had no space for Curly. He was absorbed in the movie and his legs was shaking nonstop. I patted his gluteal muscles, which were very firm. He gave me a look of disgust.

After I finished all my dinner, Curly took some sportswear out of the wardrobe and let me choose. I found that they were all Nike products. I looked at him blankly. He proudly said that Nike signed a contract with him. In the future, he could only wear Nike products, and they were all free. I checked the wardrobe: it was full of Nikes. I took out a pair of Jordan shoes and looked at Curly. He said nervously that the shoes were limited edition. I insisted on giving them a try. Curly couldn't convince me to give up and I could feel that he wasn't very willing. I wilfully ignored him. I wore the Jordans all night until it was time to go to bed. At first, we slept in a single bed because Curly didn't want to trouble his roommate's bed even though the bed was empty. We lay on our sides and watched TV. It wasn't long before he disliked the fact that I was too close to him. I was messing with him on purpose. He called me a gorilla and slept in his roommate's bed. We continued to watch TV head-to-head. We talked a lot that evening. Curly had an ambition in his heart. He said that he would become a dragon in Shanghai in the future. He told me to work hard too. If he didn't stand out in the future, he would have to rely on me. I said no problem, sincerely. As long as I had a bite to eat, I would not let him go hungry. Then I added, "I want the Jordans."

CHAPTER XVIII

My university held a registered election for faculty candidates to become deputies in the National People's Congress. The whole campus was closed for half a day. Due to there not being enough classrooms to gather students together, the whole school voted in two groups over two periods of time. After I sat in the classroom, the counsellor counted the number of students twice to make sure there were no absences.

I got a ballot as long as my middle finger and as wide as my thumb. I needed to fill in my name and ID number, so I couldn't nominate my grandpa or any other movie star. I didn't want to be a dark horse for something like that, and the election organizers had already printed the names of the candidates on the ballot.

"There are four candidates. Choose three," counsellor said. "Choose the top three."

I found that I knew the names of the top three candidates: one man was a philosophy teacher; another man was a criminal law teacher and one woman was a history teacher on the foreign legal systems. That woman... I attended her class and I felt almost in love with her. She could quiet my soul. I was willing to select her all three times, but that wouldn't help her.

"Of course, you can also recommend candidates from your heart. You can write down the names of those you nominate in the blank section below the ballot, but I don't recommend doing so," counsellor said.

Such a phony fellow. Only a few ants could fit in the margin below the ballot.

"Has everyone chosen yet?" counsellor asked. "I'm going to start collecting ballots."

The votes in our class were all up to standard. I heard that someone nominated his counsellor in another class, that's all. Who could expect creativity from a university of politics and law? I asked the most talkative person on the earth whether democracy or tyranny was good. She thought I had no idea what I was talking about. It was a waste of time to talk to me about it.

Wendy was right. I was just asking, not really interested. After she saw my sports talent, she was a little nicer to me. She told me she cursed my ankle because I wanted to show off in front of her. I smiled in a very artificial way. She went on to pretend that if I didn't believe her, there were other curses she could give me, and she listed them. It made her look a little more lovely. I stretched out my arm to show her my goose bumps and said I was so frightened.

No one knew exactly when, at some point in time, Wendy and I became almost shadows of each other. We met every day, occasionally inviting Vig. We talked on the phone every night, when I became bold enough to say anything I dared not say when we were together. Wendy's attitude was consistent. She said I was ridiculous when I suggested having a romance. With a standard score for love in her mind, I scored negative. I actually believed that there was such a standard also. I began to satisfy all her wishes. She asked me to sing; I sang. She asked me to dance; I danced. She asked me to draw a cartoon; I drew a cartoon. She suddenly wanted to see the sea, the sunset and the sunrise. I held my breath and pretended it was none of my business. I was afraid there would be unexpected mistakes as soon as I spoke.

"Are you too happy to speak?" Wendy asked. "Don't think

that I can't see the dirty thoughts flowing in your mind."

My mouth was slightly open. My eyes were cherubic.

"Stop acting! See you at the school gate at eight o 'clock tomorrow morning,'' Wendy warned. "One minute late and you're fired."

As soon as her voice quieted, she left. I called her that night. She hung up and sent me a message, *Go to bed!* I didn't fantasize too much about the beach trip. I didn't want to let my mind wander too far. The next morning, I woke up an hour earlier, before my alarm clock rang. I took my time to get my morning personal cleaning done. Then, I went to the canteen and had a leisurely breakfast. I realized I found such a morning pleasant. I used to rush like I was in a hurry when there was actually no need to be hurry. It was just for the sake of getting a little more sleep.

After my stomach was full, I strolled to the school gate. I had a hunch that Vig would join us. Maybe they formed a tour group. I shrugged and let it be.

Ten minutes to eight, Wendy appeared in front of me.

"Where is your scooter?" she asked. "Where is your bag?"

"What?"

"You want to walk to the beach?" she asked, "and you didn't prepare anything for the trip?"

"Just you and me?" I asked. "I have money in my pocket."

"Who else did you want?" she said. "If you don't want to go with me, I'll go by myself."

"Wait a moment!" I was surprised. "I don't know the way to the beach."

"I prepared the map," she said. "I'll give you five minutes, and then I'm leaving at eight o'clock. With or without you."

I didn't worry about the time of departure at all. Wendy would have waited for me anyway. I jogged to my scooter and felt a little flower blooming in my heart.

The journey to the seaside was nearly seventy kilometres. Wendy carried her big bag on her chest to create a barrier between me and her. My little dream was shattered by her in an instant. She seized my T-shirt by the waist with both hands and said, "Drive civilized and pay attention to safety."

I made a quick start and then braked sharply. Wendy was frightened and pinched her finger into my skin, but she did not exert herself. It was a warning. If I drove in the same way again, her prepared gesture would make me feel pain. I took her hand and wrapped it around me. It was the first time I touched her hand so directly. I repeated the same start and brake. Wendy merged with the scooter in the shake.

"That's the safe way to ride," I said. "Here we go!"

"You have a lot of experience," Wendy said with a hint of sarcasm. "Take advantage of girls in this way?"

"You were my first female passenger."

"You are lying!"

"I swear to god!"

Technically, Kitty was the first female to ride this scooter, but she wasn't a passenger, she was the driver. She had commented that the speedometer was fake and that there was no way this thing could get up to one hundred and twenty kilometres an hour... One hundred and three kilometres an hour was the maximum.

Along the way, I smoothly navigated all the stopping and starting. Wendy's crossed fingers lightly covered my stomach. I had an inexplicable sense of happiness. In this case, I told myself to cut the crap as much as possible in order to keep the romance. Other than talking to me while looking at the map, Wendy kept very quiet.

It was early summer. As it was a weekday and not a school holiday, it took us only an hour to drive away from the crowded city. The road to the seaside was not busy at all. The dim blue sky and grey white clouds were still pretty. The green fields stretched as far as the eye could see on both sides of the road. Maybe because the air was so clear I sneezed twice in a row. So, we took a break on the way there. I felt as if Wendy had something on her mind. Her eyes stared straight into the distance and remained motionless. After a while, I asked her what she was thinking. Her body trembled slightly and took a deep breath.

"Nothing," she squeezed out a smile. "Should we move on?"

The moment Wendy saw the sea, she began to get excited. I sped up the scooter to match her feelings. At the junction of the beach and the asphalt road, Wendy could not wait to rush to the sea. I thought she was going to take off her jeans and show me a bikini or something, but she just took off her shoes and rolled up her pants. The sea and sand in front of me didn't excite me at all. My eyes were full of dark yellow. On the contrary, it made me feel a little depressed. I walked carefully on the sand, but the sand still got into my shoes. My only relief was that the beach was almost deserted.

"Are you old before your time?" Wendy's voice rushed at me with the sound of the waves. "Moving like a turtle."

"I was shocked by the look of the sea." I explained, "This is my first time to see the sea."

"Really?" Wendy asked, "How is that possible?"

"I'm a high jumper and my coach asked us to stay out of the water."

"What absurd nonsense."

"Have you ever seen a black swimming champion?"

Wendy ignored me. She was happy to play her chasing game

with the small waves. Somehow, suddenly a picture jumped into my mind —a sea turtle tied in a plastic ring. The truth was like that… A little sea turtle accidentally stuck in a plastic ring at the waist. After many years, its body grew, but didn't break out of the plastic ring. Its body looked like the number eight.

"Is sea water really salty?" I asked aloud.

"You'll see if you try," Wendy said.

"That's a good idea." I took off my shoes and socks, pulled up my trousers and headed for the sea.

"Are you serious?" Wendy saw me holding the sea water in my palms, and said, "No one will save you if you get poisoned!"

I took a sip of the sea water.

"What do you think?"

"Really salty," I spat out as much sea water as I could. "And bitter."

"I have mineral water in my bag," she said. "Go wash your mouth."

At noon, Wendy laid out the picnic mat. She took out a box of fruit, a box of ham sausages, a box of vegetable salad, a box of sauced beef, a bag of bread and several bottles of carbonated drinks from her bag. I wondered what was left in her bag and she stopped me before I tried to see it all.

"How dare you!" She wasn't really angry. "This is a girl's bag."

"Please forgive me!" I put my hands together and pretended to apologize piously. "I just want to give you a hand."

Of course, Wendy would not accept my nonsense. She started shooting at me like a machine gun in Mandarin with a northern accent. Only when food came into her mouth would her witty words stop. To be honest, it was a pleasure to be scolded by her.

After lunch, in order to make things more comfortable, I piled the sand into a pillow shape and covered it with the picnic mat. My actions were praised by Wendy. In order to an even more comfortable effect, I adjusted the shape of the sand at the waist.

The soft sea breeze caressed my face from time to time. My body and mind felt unusually relaxed, and then I fell asleep. It was almost four o'clock in the afternoon when I opened my eyes. I felt as if I had been isolated from the outside world for a long time. I looked at Wendy drowsily. She was reading a book and didn't know I was awake. Her profile was so beautiful, like Mona Lisa. I sucked the air in my lung and yawned.

"You were a pig in your last life," Wendy didn't take her eyes off the book. "You snore like a pig."

"Really?" I scratched my head. "Strangely, I've never snored before."

"It's a pity that I don't have a recorder," she said.

"What book are you reading?" I asked.

Wendy turned the cover of the book to me. I saw a strange title, *The Catcher in the Rye*. I wondered what the book was about.

"A boy's story," Wendy said. "You should read it."

"When are we leaving?" I asked.

"After sunrise."

"After sunset," I said to myself. "That's all right."

"After sunrise." Wendy shifted her eyes from the book to my face.

"What?" My expression was puzzled. "You want to spend the night here?"

"Why not?"

"You'll freeze to death on this beach."

"Who told you that I was going to spend the night on the

beach?"

"I am totally confused." I was lying on my side with one hand holding my head and looking at her.

"Have you heard of a place in the world called..." Wendy slowed down and said word by word, "A hotel?"

"Holy shit! No ID card with me." I jumped up, "Why didn't you say that earlier?"

Wendy pretended not to hear.

"You wait for me here," I said. "I'll be back soon."

"Are you taking a helicopter?" Wendy asked.

"Don't worry," I said. "I won't be gone more than two hours."

"You stop!" Wendy said in a very serious voice. "First of all, it's impossible to get back and forth within two hours. It's going to be rush hour soon. Second, don't you think it's dangerous to leave a young and beauty girl like me waiting here alone?"

"Oh, sorry, let me take you to the hotel first."

"No!" Wendy said, "I want to watch the sunset here!"

I moved my hips back to the picnic mat. For the rest of the time, neither of us spoke. The colours of the sun ranged from light yellow to orange, gradually turning to light red. The clouds were like flaming torches. The sun slowly sank toward the sea level. The colour of the sky changed from light purple to deep blue. The sky was getting darker and darker. The sound of the waves hitting the shore became clearer and clearer.

I drove Wendy to the hotel where she wanted to go. She asked me to sit in the corner of the hotel lobby. I watched her check in, and then I received a text message. She was asking me to follow her and not look around. I suddenly felt more nervous than ever. I controlled my breathing and walked as calmly as I could. She disappeared around the corner. I quickened my pace a little and saw that she was blocking the elevator door with her hand.

Up to the sixth floor, I followed her, keeping a distance of two metres. She opened a door, and I flashed into the room like a thief without being able to even steal a glance at the room number. As soon as I entered the room, I laid face down on the bed and heard the door closed.

"Get up!" Wendy said. "Do you think you'll be the one sleeping in that bed?"

"Why didn't you take a twin room then?" I actually knew why.

"You are a rascal!" Wendy said. "I warn you, do not have any delusions."

"I'll sleep in the bathroom!" I got up and said.

"Don't betray my trust!" Wendy's eyes were full of seriousness. I felt it would be almost impossible to get her to trust me, so I made an impassioned speech to prove that I was a gentleman. I was in a really good mood, so I used many vows to strengthen my sincerity. At the end, I told her that it was unrealistic to sleep in the bathroom. I would put the picnic mat on the floor and sleep on that. Wendy opened the backpack and threw the picnic mat at me. I spread it on the floor next to the window. Through the top left of the window, there was a lighthouse.

"What a starry sky!" I faced the glass window with my hands on my cheeks and asked, "What shall we have for dinner?"

"How can you... How can you associate the nightscape with eating?"

"Because my stomach is growling."

"What a romantic guy!"

"I've always thought about how easy it would be if human

beings would be like plants, needing only air, water and sunshine."

"Please go forage some food by yourself." Wendy directed. "The door is there. The legs you can find on the bottom half of your body."

I took the scooter key out of my trouser pocket, weighed it twice in the palm of my hand, making a metal collision sound, and walked towards the door to look through the peephole. I had no intention of leaving the room, even if it would mean I would starve to death. After all, I was an unregistered person. I didn't want to make Wendy nervous, because I didn't think she was. Actually, I was just learning how to entertain myself. In fact, she was very cooperative with my acting. She came up and held the door handle. Thanks to my quick reaction, I held the door closed with my knee.

"What are you doing?" I asked in a low voice.

"If you want to leave," Wendy raised her voice, "please, hurry up!"

"Who said I was leaving?" I kept my voice low and pushed her back to the window.

"Aren't you hungry?" Wendy was still in soprano mode.

"Keep your voice down!"

"Why?"

"Civilized accommodation," I said. "Don't disturb the neighbours with noise."

All of sudden, Wendy seemed to become a double character. She threw the pillow at me and asked me to return it. She asked me to stand on one leg with a pillow on my head until she announced she was tired. If I didn't satisfy her command, she warned, opening her mouth to show me her teeth, she was ready to scream. In order to cooperate with her, I pretended to jump up in fright, and then I landed on one leg with a pillow on my head, shaking left and right several times. Finally, she showed that she was hungry, but by then my hunger had given up on me. We each ate a bowl of instant noodles from the hotel. I also ate the leftovers from the picnic. I suggested Wendy to go to the supermarket and buy two more boxes of the same instant noodles, to replace the hotel's. Besides, we needed some snacks and soft drinks. She readily agreed. I took the opportunity to say that I needed six more cans of beer. She also very readily agreed and asked me what kind of beer. In order not to make things too complicated, I pointed to the beer on display in the hotel and then opened a can to drink.

Then I was alone in the room. I was thinking, as a man, I should take the initiative, but I didn't know what I should do. My mind was so muddled that I could not come up with any plan at all. I thought that I should kiss Wendy, but under what circumstances, in what atmosphere, how to go about it… I had no idea. I ended up feeling like Wendy was the one who was in complete control of what would happen. I thought, if she wanted a kiss, she would give me enough hints. All I needed to do was brush my teeth.

I drank nearly a dozen beers that night. My last memory was that Wendy gave me a long kiss. When I woke up, my body was in bed and my clothes were on me. Wendy had disappeared. I looked at my phone. It was almost noon. There was a message from Wendy: *I'm back in university. When you wake up, close the door and leave. Drive safely. Last night, you drank too much, but nothing happened. I left a note in the bathroom.* The time stamp of the message was around nine a.m.

The note in the bathroom said: *If I had met you earlier, I don't know what would have happened. We are strangers when we meet again. Don't ask me why. Please respect my decision.*

CHAPTER XIX

That's pretty much all I want to say for now. Later, I fell in love with a girl from the same city as me. She was my first official girlfriend. I wasn't ready to write out that story, because she had a powerful father and she warned me not to write about her in a novel unless I was ready to emigrate to Mars.

I did meet Wendy several times on campus. At first, she pretended not to see me. I watched her pass by. Later, I pretended not to see her. She was staring at my girlfriend. It caused me a little trouble. My girlfriend was as sensitive as an antenna and would be jealous for no reason.

In the third year of college, I almost joined the army. Because it was the first time, they were recruiting college students to serve as soldiers, the government promised many attractive incentives. My determination was laughed at by my girlfriend's father. So, I didn't go. But if I had…

But in life, there are no ifs.

Actually, I don't know myself very well. I always thought I knew everything. Looking back, it is just a faint smile.